ALSO BY TALIA HIBBERT

RAVENSWOOD

A Girl Like Her

Damaged Goods, a bonus novella

Untouchable

That Kind of Guy

DIRTY BRITISH ROMANCE

The Princess Trap

Wanna Bet?

JUST FOR HIM

Bad for the Boss

Undone by the Ex-Con

Sweet on the Greek

STANDALONE TITLES

Merry Inkmas

Mating the Huntress

Operation Atonement

Always With You

DAMAGED
GOODS

Ravenswood Book 1.5

TALIA HIBBERT

Nixon House

Published by Nixon House.

ISBN: 978-1-9164043-1-1

For Truly Scrumptious, my blessing.

CONTENT NOTE

Please be aware: this book contains descriptions of domestic abuse, intimate partner violence, and child abuse that may trigger some readers. Specific warnings below.

- Chapter 5: Detailed discussion of child abuse.
- Chapter 9: Depiction of domestic abuse and intimate partner violence.
- Chapter 12: Gaslighting and internalised misogyny.
- Chapter 16: Confrontation with abuser and gaslighting.
- Chapter 18: Depiction of childbirth.

CHAPTER ONE

THE STRANGER ARRIVED on a Saturday night.

Her great, sleek Range Rover rumbled into the seaside village, gleaming like whale skin under the full moon. A young lad walking his dog watched it pass in awe, his jaw slack. Not even during the season, when the middle-classes descended upon Beesley-On-Sea for their summer holidays, had he seen such extravagant rims on a car. And he'd certainly never come across a private plate like that.

BURN3, it read.

The car drove past the astonished youth without pause. Its driver barely saw the boy, just as she'd barely seen the *Welcome to Beesley-on-Sea!* sign she'd passed five minutes ago. It didn't matter, though; she knew exactly where she was. Even after all these years, the briny tang of seawater on the breeze made her muscles loosen and her heart rise. By the time she reached her destination, the old beach house, she was grinning like a ninny.

The driver's name was Laura, and she left her rings in the glovebox.

They were irritating, anyway, you see. The teardrop diamond of her engagement ring always dug into her other fingers. The wedding band was alright—if one forgot the part where it symbolised her legal attachment to the biggest piece of shit on earth. But, she reminded herself, that attachment would soon be dissolved. Thank fuck.

The beach house of Laura's memory was a grand old thing, but fifteen years later it was simply… well, an *old* thing. Her father-in-law's monstrous Range Rover looked ridiculous on the driveway, gleaming smugly beside the house's battered wood panelling and chipped, white window frames. And yet, in an instant, she loved the beach house quite unreasonably. The car she loved far less, even if it *had* allowed her madcap escape.

The house keys had been left in the old post-box by the door, because the estate agent overseeing this rent was an older, small-town man. The older, small-town man, Laura knew, was a curious specimen. They tended to lack the proper survival instincts, so they did ridiculous things like… well, like leaving the keys to a house in said house's post-box and trusting that no-one would steal them.

Thankfully, no-one had. Laura glanced over her shoulder as she fished them out, squinting into the moonlit darkness, searching for potential home invaders. All she saw was leafy isolation across the street and scattered stars lighting up the night. All she heard were the familiar sounds of night creatures hooting and rustling and whispering on the breeze. She could almost pretend she was back home in Ravenswood.

But not quite. There were three key differences, so far, between Ravenswood and Beesley. The first: Ravenswood didn't have a beach, and thus its breeze lacked the raw, wild, salty scent of Beesley's. The second: in Ravenswood, she would've been secure in the knowledge that her friends—or at the very least, her father-in-law—were within walking distance. The third: she would also have been terrified by the knowledge that her *husband* was within walking distance.

That last point alone made Beesley far preferable to Ravenswood right now. She hurried into the house.

Its interior was as charmingly faded as its exterior had been, filled with mismatched furniture and outdated appliances. Laura hadn't brought much with her, so it didn't take long to unpack. Everything had its place: designer clothes stuffed into the bleached-wood wardrobe, La Mer arranged on the eighties-style tiles of the en-suite's counter, phone charger plugged in by the dusty-rose divan. She wandered downstairs, stomach growling, and found the kitchen fully stocked.

The sight of fat, round grapes by the sink, a floury bloomer in the pantry, and a slab of white cheese in the fridge made Laura nauseous. This was the food she'd requested. This was the food that, five minutes ago, she'd been desperate to shovel down her throat. Now the mere idea made her stomach roil. The midwife's pamphlets had totally lied, and Laura was still bitter about it. Morning—or evening, or afternoon, or *midnight*—sickness did not fade after the first trimester.

"Alright then," she murmured, looking down at the swell of her stomach. "What do you fancy?"

The bump remained silent. *Typical.*

She wandered over to the kitchen sink and ran her sweaty palms over its cool steel. Still fighting the queasy lurch in her gut, Laura glanced out of the window at the stars, then studied the narrow scrap of beach outside, untouched by the high tide.

That was the ocean she saw, winking at her like an old flirt, just beyond the sand. Oh, how she loved the ocean.

"A walk on the beach, perhaps?" she suggested to her own abdomen.

The foetus within held its tongue. Did they have tongues, at this stage? She'd have to consult her pamphlets again.

Oh, whatever. The baby may not have an opinion, but Laura knew exactly what she wanted.

And for the first time in a while, she was free to go for it.

SAMIR DIDN'T *THINK* he was being spied on.

On the one hand, people were often spied on here in Beesley—especially during the off-season. Folks had too much damned time on their hands. The elderly in particular became vampires in their old age, always thirsty for someone else's drama.

But on the other hand, whoever had just joined him on the beach was far too noisy to be a spy. Surely, if they were trying to be sneaky, they wouldn't blunder over the stony shoreline like the world's loudest bulldozer. And they certainly wouldn't be tossing pebbles into the silky ink of the ocean with a successive *plop, plop, plop* that yanked him right out of his evening's angst-fest.

So they weren't going to pinch his cheek and call him a lovely boy, and they weren't going to tell the whole town that Samir Bianchi had been staring out to sea, grim-faced and resentful, like some wannabe Batman. Those were good things. Very good things.

But Samir still wasn't feeling charitable toward the person who'd intruded on his solitude—and never mind the fact that this was a public beach. It was the middle of the night, for goodness's sake. A man should be able to brood without interruption on a beach in the middle of the night. An hour or two of self-indulgence wasn't asking for much.

Clearly the bulldozer disagreed. They came ever closer, ever louder, ever clumsier, until it became suddenly and painfully clear that Samir was going to have to announce his presence. It was dark enough that, if he didn't, this bulldozer of a human being might just bulldoze him.

"Hey," he said, his voice breaking the gentle, wave-tinged silence.

"Argh!" the bulldozer said and fell on top of him.

What followed was an alarming series of shrieks, grunts and mumbled apologies that Samir really could've done without.

"Bloody hell," he blurted as the bulldozer collapsed over him like a sack of bricks.

"Oh!" the bulldozer cried. "I'm so sorry!" She—it did *seem* to be a she—accompanied those words with what felt like a shoulder to his throat.

"Bloody *hell!*" he spluttered, this time with even greater feeling.

A small storm of sand was kicked up as the two of them shuffled apart like crabs on speed. He felt the grit against his skin, scratching his dry eyes, and even sneaking into his open, panting mouth. *Delightful.*

Eventually, despite all the scuffling and swearing and shrieking—this bulldozer operated at a rather high pitch— they managed to put a decent amount of space between them. Samir could see the outline of a person in the moonlight, just a few feet away. The gentle *whoosh* of the wind over the waves should've made the silence between them peaceful. Instead, it felt painfully awkward. He should say something, really. The only problem was, he thought his voice box might be damaged. The woman's shoulder must be made of bloody brick.

"I'm sorry," she said, the words sudden and disarmingly earnest. She sounded absolutely mortified. In fact, it was more than that; she sounded ready to throw herself down a well. The abject discomfort in her voice was so intense, it was making *him* uncomfortable. And there was something else, too—something in her tone, or maybe her accent, that tugged at a thread in the back of his mind. It was a weird sensation.

He decided to ignore it.

"It's okay," he managed, his voice far too cracked and hoarse to be convincing. "Don't worry about it."

She snorted. It was a soft, horse-like sound, and something about it tugged on that thread again. "It most certainly is *not* okay," she said. "I must've squashed you."

This was the part where he lied gallantly. "I wouldn't say *squashed*—"

"*I* would."

"It wasn't that bad."

"I might believe you," she said wryly, "if you weren't still wheezing like a donkey."

Samir managed to choke out a laugh in between wheezes.

Maybe his eyes were adjusting, or maybe some of the cloud cover had passed. Whatever the reason, he suddenly caught a glimpse of his strange companion: the gleam of moonlight on long, dark hair as she tipped her head back; the outline of a sharp, rather no-nonsense nose; the curve of the impressively substantial shoulder that had found its way to his throat. No wonder he was still a bit winded.

"Please," she said, sounding oddly, subtly urgent. "Let me be sorry. I'm very, very sorry."

He recognised something in her voice—something self-flagellating and hopeful all at once. Something he'd heard in his own voice, once upon a time. Or rather, he *thought* he did. He was probably imagining things.

"If it matters so much," he said lightly, "you can be as sorry as you like."

"Oh, thank you," she murmured, a slight smile in her voice. "I appreciate it."

And wasn't the human mind such a strange thing? Because, out of everything she'd said over the past five minutes, it was that single phrase—those three little words —that pulled loose the insistent, tugging thread in his mind.

"*I appreciate it,*" she'd said fifteen years ago, after he'd given her a stolen Cornetto. She'd been all prim and proper while she unwrapped his ill-gotten goods, and for some reason it had made his teenaged heart sing. He'd wanted to steal a thousand more Cornettos, just for her.

Over the course of the summer, he probably had.

Samir sank his fingers into the gritty sand, grounding himself even as strange hope ran wild. Surely not. *Surely* not. This woman, whoever she was, dredged up old memories for some other reason. She just happened to have the same accent and that same arch tone. It was a coincidence. Because the chances of meeting *her* again, here, after all this time…

It wasn't possible. That sort of thing didn't happen.

But Samir found himself squinting at her in the darkness, anyway, as if he could will himself to develop night vision.

"Are you okay?" she asked. She might as well have whacked him over the head. *Now* he was sure. He was positive. He could've predicted every inflection in that sentence, from the way she glided over the *you* to the wobbling lilt on *okay*, as if she really gave a shit. Because she did.

"Laura?" he asked slowly. And, though he'd been certain a second ago, just saying her name made it seem so impossible. Made him think that he must be mistaken.

Until she stilled, her shadowy outline stiffening. Her voice was hard as glass and twice as fragile when she demanded, "Who are you?"

Because of course she'd be freaked out by a strange man knowing her name. Who wouldn't? Through the flood of disbelief rushing over him, he managed to say, "It's Samir. Samir Bianchi. Do you remember me?"

For a single, stuttering heartbeat, he thought the answer might be *no*. But then she spoke, sounding as astonished as he felt. "Samir? Seriously?

It was her.

CHAPTER TWO

"HOLY SHIT," Samir said.

Samir. *Samir.* Her mind couldn't quite take that part in.

His incredulous laughter was as bright as the few stars beaming through the clouds. "Laura Albright. I'm sitting on a beach with *Laura Albright.* Again. What the fuck?"

Laura almost jumped out of her skin when he said her maiden name. *Albright.* It sounded good. Perfect, in fact. Like summer nights and freedom. Like before. Like herself.

"I can't believe this," she murmured, sounding like some high school reunion cliché. But this was way beyond school reunion shit, because Samir had never belonged to the mundane world of home and studying and sensible behaviour. Samir had been her six-week rebellion. Samir had been everything.

"What are you *doing* here?" he asked. The force of his attention cut through the dark, just like she remembered. She *felt* it—but not like the weight of her husband's insatiable eyes. Not even like the spotlight she lived under back home, where folks brightened the stage so they could spot any false moves. Any mistakes. Any weakness.

No; this was pure, honest interest, the kind that made you feel *interesting*. And she wasn't used to it at all.

"I… well," she said, stumbling over her words. "I'm having a baby."

She didn't have to see him to know he'd faltered or hear him to realise he was shocked. There was a slight pause before he said, "Wow. That's amazing. *Wow.* Congratulations!"

"Thanks," she said, even though she didn't feel like being congratulated. She hadn't really achieved anything. In fact, she'd failed her kid already, falling pregnant by a man like Daniel.

But that was a negative thought, and she had decided to avoid those. Positivity was better for the baby.

"Are you staying at the house?" Samir asked. "Like you used to? Is your family here?"

"Yes, and no. I mean, I'm at the beach house, but no-one's here. Oh, Dad died, actually. Ages ago. I don't know how much you remember him." They'd only been here six weeks, after all. A single summer holiday, during which her parents spent their time getting wasted, as always, and Laura had watched her little sister, as always.

And yet, it had been nothing like always. All because of Samir Bianchi.

"Oh, shit," he said. "That's rough. I'm sorry."

"Eh. His liver. Not like it was a surprise." She hesitated, slightly guilty about her own dispassionate tone. "It shook Mum up, though. She's sober now."

"Huh." There was a short pause that threatened to be awkward. Then Samir said, "So is she still an insufferable cow, or was that just the alcohol?"

Laura shouldn't have laughed. If she were a good, respectful, *sensitive* daughter, she wouldn't have laughed. But she hadn't been good, respectful, or sensitive for a long time, so she practically pissed herself.

"Oh my God," she wheezed, when she could finally catch her breath. "Jesus. You're so unbelievable."

"I'm just asking the question on everybody's mind, angel."

"No-one else is *here*, Samir."

"My mind, then. Whatever." She could hear that old, infectious grin in his voice, charming as ever. God, she couldn't believe she hadn't recognised him—even in the dark, even when all he'd done was grunt and swear and be fallen on. Surely, she should've known him. Surely, she should've known her first kiss, her first love, her first *everything*. The only person who'd ever made her understand the phrase *best friend*.

But it had been a while, and she wasn't the person she used to be. He probably wasn't either. And yet, he seemed so painfully familiar.

"Both my parents died," he said, "if we're doing a family roll-call. Car crash."

"Oh, my God. Fuck. I'm so sorry."

He snorted. "Either you've forgotten everything about my parents, or you're lying through your teeth."

She was glad he couldn't see her lips twitching. "I'm being respectful of the dead."

"Don't bother. I'm actually out here celebrating."

"What?!"

"Well, it was five years ago today. And I was feeling especially belligerent, so I came out to brood. You know how my mother hated brooding."

"Oh, yes," she said solemnly, as if she couldn't hear the teasing in his voice. "I remember." Because really, his mother had hated everything. *Anything.* Whatever her children did, she'd disapproved of.

The worst thing about Samir's parents—worse than the cruelty, the manipulation, the toxicity—was the fact that Samir had loved them. Unlike Laura, he didn't see his parents as pathetic fuck-ups. He wanted to please them.

But they would never be pleased.

So if he really was out here to celebrate... well, maybe she should be horrified, but really, she was glad. She hoped that he finally hated their guts. It was the very least they deserved.

"How's your brother?" she asked, just to say something.

"Hassan? Boring. Married. He and his husband are in the RAF, can you believe that? They're stationed in the Falklands."

"Really? Military?" She wrinkled her nose. Samir's twin had been, if possible, even wilder than him.

"Yeah; he says it helps with his temper. The order keeps him calm. "

"What keeps you calm?"

"Frequent masturbation," he said dryly.

It was a totally Samir thing to say. It was the sort of statement that had made her half-terrified, half-intrigued when they'd met as fifteen-year-olds. She'd never known anyone so casually outrageous, someone who said whatever came into his head and only wanted to make other people smile. But now, for some reason, the sharp honesty didn't make her giggle. It made her swallow, hard, and clear her throat, and fidget awkwardly in the sand.

He must have sensed her discomfort, because he laughed and said, "Sorry. I still have a questionable filter."

"You don't *have* a filter," she replied, a slow smile tilting her lips. She was probably blushing like a tomato right now.

"Very true. And since we've established that—would it be rude of me to ask who knocked you up?"

She snorted, laughter bubbling up without permission. "Someone with the necessary equipment."

"*Someone* sounds quite distant."

"Well, he's far away from here. So distant is right."

"Hmm." Samir's air of constant amusement cooled, solidifying between them. She barely had time to wonder at the change before he said, "Just to clarify—is he distant because you want him to be, or because he's a piece of shit?"

"Um… both?"

There was a pause. Then, his voice gentler now, he asked, "Laura… are you here on your own?"

"Yes," she admitted. "It's not a big deal. I wanted to come alone."

He ignored that completely. "For how long?"

"I told you," she said, trying not to sound self-conscious. "I'm having a baby."

"Assume I know nothing about human gestation, since I don't. How long?"

"I'm due in September. Mum and Hayley are coming eventually—you know, in the last few weeks or so…"

He sighed heavily. Her eyes tracked the motion of his

shadowy outline, and she couldn't be sure, but she *thought* he was raking a hand through his hair. It was a familiar motion, one she remembered even after fifteen years. Just like she remembered exactly how that hair felt, thick and soft and swirling from his crown in unruly waves.

"We haven't seen each other in years," he said. "*Years*. We don't… we don't really know each other anymore. Technically."

Something in her instinctively wanted to disagree with that, after ten minutes catching up on a beach in the dark. Which was ridiculous. The little things, the surface things about him, might seem the same, but he must be different now. *She* was different now. She was a little bit ruined.

She was damaged.

"I don't want to act like we're still close," he said. She thought it was unusually tactful of him to say *close* instead of what they'd actually been. But then, what they'd actually been was the sort of thing that didn't matter as much at thirty as it had at fifteen.

"I'm not going to storm into your life and act like your guard dog," he muttered, and she realised that he was actually talking to himself. *Convincing* himself.

"You're not?" she asked, an edge of mischief in her voice. She hadn't heard that edge in a long time. It was a shock, to have it back all of a sudden—but a good one.

"No," he said wryly. "I'm not. That would be out of order."

"Okay. But if you *were* going to do such a thing—"

"See, everyone always called you the good girl, but I knew from the start you'd be a bad influence."

"If you *were*," she repeated with a grin, "what would you say right now?"

He heaved out another of those sighs. "I'd say I have a cafe in town called Bianchi's. And you should come and see me tomorrow. And tell me about this guy with the necessary equipment and the bad attitude."

At the thought of sullying Samir's ears with even the whisper of Daniel's name, panic stung her like a jellyfish gliding out of deep waters. "I can't do that," she said, her throat suddenly tight. "I mean—he's—I can't talk about him. You're—and he's—I don't want to talk about him—"

"Laura," Samir said, his voice achingly gentle. She felt his hand bump into her upper arm, and then her shoulder... and then, finally, he pushed her hair out of the way and rested his palm against the back of her neck. Just like he used to. "It's okay," he said. "Don't worry. We can talk about whatever you want—about something else. Anything else. Okay?" He squeezed slightly, and she realised that her breath was coming fast. "Okay?"

"Yeah," she managed. "Cool. Yeah. Something else. Sorry —I'm kind of on edge. Long day."

"I get it," he murmured. His hand left her as quickly as it had come, and she shouldn't have felt like she'd just lost something.

She did, though.

Even worse, as her panic drained away, embarrassment rose to take its place. Jesus. She'd just hyperventilated at the mention of her husband.

Ex-husband.

Ex-husband-to-be.

Oh, she was so sick of thinking about this.

But then Samir said, "Hey, do you remember when we convinced Hayley that me and Hassan were the same person?"

All of a sudden, she wasn't thinking about Daniel at all.

CHAPTER THREE

SAMIR'S CAFE wasn't hard to miss. For one thing, he had a spot of prime real estate on Beesley-on Sea's main promenade. For another, the shop's sign was basically an enormous Italian flag. It stood out amongst the cobbled streets, to say the least. Laura smirked as she entered the cafe's propped-open door. God, he was so annoying. He wasn't even *that* Italian.

And why was she thinking about him like that? As if she knew him? As if it had been a week since they'd last spoken instead of fifteen years? She couldn't let herself get too comfortable, regardless of their history. Getting comfortable with men usually ended in tears.

Laura's hand drifted down to cup her stomach as she wandered toward the cafe's counter. There was a woman standing there, tapping at the till. If Laura was her old self, Daniel's Laura, she'd say that the woman's over-bleached hair looked like straw and the turquoise eyeliner bleeding into her crow's feet was giving off *Braveheart* vibes. But

Laura was herself now, not some pathetic, wounded creature lashing out at anyone who passed by, wielding preemptive cruelty as a shield. She'd come here to get her shit together and become mother material. So she should think instead that the woman's French braid was cute, and that her fuchsia lipstick made her teeth look whiter.

Actually, Laura shouldn't think anything at all. She shouldn't *be* here. She should be taking long, scenic walks through the town's wooded trails, or booking back-to-back spa appointments with the town's only beautician, or reading the literal mountain of self-help books still sitting in the Range Rover's boot. Sensible things, in short, that didn't involve gallivanting around after men. Right?

Right. Definitely. In fact, the siren song of boring behaviour grew so strong that she actually turned to leave.

And almost walked right into Samir.

Oh, Christ. Samir.

If she'd seen him last night, even just a little bit, she'd have known him in seconds. How could she not, when he was still so beautiful? Amber skin, chaotic, midnight hair, eyes dark and warm as hot chocolate. When they were young, she'd been an inch taller than him. Now he towered over her, and he was broader, too. He might even be bigger than Daniel.

But she wouldn't think about Daniel.

There were other differences. His face had been finer, almost delicate, before, but now it teetered between lush and brutish. His nose was crooked, but his mouth was soft and wide as ever. And when he grinned... oh, there was nothing different about that. His smile was a slice of sunshine. It was the sort of smile that promised he'd give you anything, do anything for you, just to make you happy. That *he'd* be happy to do it. He was that kind of guy.

"Damn," he said, his gaze raking over her body. For a moment, Laura felt this odd, tingling flush that she hadn't felt in forever, the sort that lit her up like a power surge. But then he said, "You really *are* pregnant," and the power winked out with a *pop*.

"That's what they tell me," she said cheerfully, while her brain melted through sheer embarrassment. Of course, he hadn't been looking at her like *that*. Why would he? And if he had, she would've been outraged, anyway. Horrified. Disgusted! She might even have slapped him. Gently, but still. The sentiment would've been there.

The woman behind the counter took her pen out from between her teeth and gave a dramatic gasp. "Samir Bianchi," she snapped, eyes narrowing until they were just glints of blue. "*What* did you just say to this poor girl?"

"What?" Samir gave the woman a look of confusion. "What did I do now?"

"You called her *pregnant*," the woman said, as if he'd actually called Laura *ugly* or *demented* or *French*.

"She *is* pregnant, Kelly."

Would anyone notice if Laura just quietly ran away?

Probably. She let her face fall into her hands, instead.

"You're not supposed to *say* so, you bloody idiot. You're supposed to say she's barely showing! You're supposed to say you can't tell at all! Good Lord. Men!"

The woman—Kelly—seemed to have completed her speech. After a moment, Laura peeked through her fingers, just to check if the floor was making any progress on the whole *opening up to swallow her* thing.

Sadly, it was not.

"Hey," Samir said, catching one of her wrists. He tugged her hand gently away from her face and murmured, "Sorry. That's Kelly. She's nosy."

"I can *hear* you, you know."

He grinned, but didn't look in the direction of the voice. "I only keep her around cuz she's married to my best friend."

"Outrageous!" Kelly hollered.

The cafe's patrons seemed unperturbed by this entire exchange. Laura got the feeling it happened a lot.

"Just so you know," Samir said, "I meant that in a good way. You know, like, well done! There's a baby in there! Sharing your oxygen! You look great."

That last sentence was sudden and blunt enough to make her blush, heat prickling across her chest. Jesus, she was blushing a lot recently. Must be a pregnancy thing. "Thanks," she said, hopefully sounding like the epitome of cool, instead of a tomato with vocal chords—which she totally was.

"Don't thank me. Come and sit down."

"Um... Okay?"

His grip on her wrist loosened, and for a moment she worried that he might let go.

Well, not *worried*. It would've been fine if he'd let go. Definitely.

But he didn't, in the end. His palm slid down to meet hers, and then, somehow, they were holding hands. He led her to the back of the cafe, skirting past cute little tables with piles of seashells at their centres, towing her like a rowboat. She stepped over a sleeping guide dog as Samir said to its owner, "Give up yet, Bex?"

The woman sitting by the dog clicked her tongue. "Piss off. I'll have it by tomorrow, I bet."

"We'll see." They reached a row of cream-and-red leather booths, and Samir slid in on one side as Laura took the other. Lowering his voice, he leaned over the table and explained, "We have this weekly riddle competition. It's complicated. She thinks she's smarter than me."

"*Is* she smarter than you?" Laura whispered back.

"Depends on who you ask. But, just between us, God, yes."

Laura laughed, leaning back against the booth's soft cushions. "You know, this is cool. This whole place." And it was. If she remembered correctly, last time she'd been in Beesley, this lot had been a typical, greasy seaside cafe. Now it was a pretty, *clean* seaside cafe with a wonderful smell emanating from the kitchen and Samir's name on the menus. She wondered exactly how that had come to pass. She wondered a lot of things about Samir, actually. But she wasn't quite sure how to go about getting answers.

She should've known he'd make it easy for her, though. He always had.

"Thanks," he grinned. "You know what? I worked my arse off for years, saving up so I could open a place like this. And I was so fucking close. Then my parents died and left us about twice as much as I'd saved." He rolled his eyes. "Sod's law. Worked out great, really. But we're not here to talk about me, are we?"

"I don't know," she said nervously. "Couldn't we be here to talk about you? I'd like to talk about you."

He looked at her for a minute—just looked, dark eyes drilling into her in a way that dragged her back through time. He'd always had this ability to know, behind all his laughter and irreverent charm, when it was time to be serious. Apparently, he still had the knack, because his voice gentled and he said, "You don't need to worry, angel. I'm not going to grill you or anything. I just want to catch up."

She wet her lips nervously. "Okay. Cool."

"You want a drink? Shit, I should've gotten you a drink. Are you hungry?"

"Um... no," she lied, "I'm fine. Don't worry about it."

He snorted. "You're a horrible liar. Five minutes of looking after a pregnant woman and I'm already starving you. You want an omelette?"

"You're not looking after me," she said indignantly.

He arched a brow as if to say, *that's what you think.* "Clearly I'm doing a piss-poor job of it. Omelette; yes, no, other?"

"Um... well, I wouldn't say no to an omelette, actually. With ham. And cheese. And maybe some chips. And a salad," she added, even though she didn't want a salad at all. Vitamins were good for the baby, so she made it her mission to stuff down as many green things as possible.

"Coming up," he said, sliding out of the booth with a wink.

Oh dear. Oh *dear.*

She really, really wished he hadn't winked.

SAMIR STUCK his head through the little window that separated cafe from kitchen and called in to Max, "Ham and cheese omelette with everything."

Max looked up from the hissing hob, whiskey-brown eyes sharp. "Where's the ticket?"

"No ticket."

His face split into a grin. "Ah. Would this be for your lady friend, then?"

"Jesus. Do you and Kelly do anything other than talk?"

"Oh, yes," Max said, eyes dancing. "We do *lots* of other things. Like—"

"*At work*," Samir said hastily. "I meant at work. You know what? Never mind. Keep your grand passion to yourself. Filthy old man."

Max snorted. "Get your head out of my kitchen, Bianchi."

"Yes, Sir." With a mocking salute, he turned toward the coffee machine, where Kelly's eldest daughter, Daisy, was pretending to make a cappuccino while texting under her apron. Ingenious, really.

Of course, the ingenuity didn't stop Samir from pulling the teenager's ponytail and saying, "Turn it off or I'm telling your dad." See, Samir may be the café's owner, but lanky, bald-headed Max seemed to be the one all the staff deferred to. Go figure. Daisy gave him a kohl-lined glare, but there was little venom to it. *His* teenage glares could've stopped hearts. Or so he liked to think.

"Be cool, Uncle Samir," she mumbled.

"Too old to be cool. Instead of wasting my fancy coffee beans, you can bring two glasses of water and some orange juice to table nineteen." He enjoyed her look of outrage as he plucked the unfinished cappuccino from her hands. It looked halfway decent. He gave it an experimental sniff as he walked away, ignoring Daisy's resentful mutterings. Fuck it. Coffee was coffee. He took a sip.

When he returned to their table, Laura was pouring over the menu like it was *Lord of the Rings.*

He slid into place opposite her and said, "What do you think?"

She looked up, and the smile on her face was like an arrow to the chest. Not his *heart,* exactly. It just sort of winded him, how brilliant she was. How her cheeks were still all sweet and round, and her hair was still long and straight as ribbon, and she still had all those freckles on her arms but not on her face.

He hadn't looked anywhere else but her arms and her face, obviously. Those were the safe zones. The rest of her, as he'd realised with his very first glance, was decidedly *unsafe* to look at.

But he wasn't going to think about that. She was pregnant, and pregnant people were like the Pope, right? You had to treat them with total respect, even in your own head, just in case God was watching.

"I have one complaint," she said playfully, tapping the laminated plastic in her hand. "There's an Italian flag on this menu, Bianchi, but I'm not seeing any Italian food."

"Ah, come on!" he grinned. "It's a seaside cafe. You want me to put bruschetta on the menu, or what?"

"I'm just saying. Seems like false advertising..."

"There's nothing Moroccan on the menu, either."

"But you didn't put a Moroccan flag on the menu," she shot back. "If you did, I'd be demanding Moroccan food, too."

"What if there weren't any flags on the menu at all? Could I only serve recipes devised in international waters? Because I think I'm up to that challenge."

When she laughed, something inside him slotted into place. As if making her laugh was part of his life's work, somehow. As if this was what he should've been doing all along.

Maybe it was.

CHAPTER FOUR

"Guess who's in town?"

"Do I give a shit?" Hassan sounded irritated, but that didn't faze Samir. Hassan always sounded irritated.

"Sure, you do. It's Laura Albright."

The pause on the other end of the line was quite satisfying. Samir grinned, settling into the worn, leather chair behind the desk that dominated his office. A folder of invoices sat by his computer, waiting to be filed, but talking to his brother was far more important than keeping the accountant's bill down.

"Well, fuck," Hassan said finally. "You're joking."

"Would I lie?"

"Lie? Never. Take the absolute piss? Yes."

Samir rolled his eyes. "Do you think I'm joking, then? Tell me. Really." Because one person Samir could never fool was his twin.

Another pause. And then Hassan said slowly, "I think you're dead serious. You talked to her?"

"Of course!" Samir's smile felt too wide for his face. "We met at the beach last night—by accident, but what are the chances? She's so different, now. But the same. Does that make sense? She asked about you."

Hassan laughed, which was rare enough to command instant attention. Then he said, "I should've known this would happen eventually. Fate wouldn't have it any other way."

The words were confusing in themselves, but something about the tone of his brother's voice set off an alarm inside Samir's head. Not the *danger* siren; more the uneasy whine that meant, *tread carefully*. Frowning, he asked, "What's that supposed to mean?"

Hassan, as always, didn't hold back. "We *are* talking about Laura Albright, the love of your life, right?"

Samir's brows shot up. "*What?*"

"You heard me."

"What's in the water over there?" he chuckled. "Tell me, really; have you signed up for any military experiments, recently? Anything that might scramble your brain, I mean?"

Hassan's reply was typically unamused. "Shut up. You're calling me because the object of your affections has returned, and you don't know how to deal with your reawakened love. Do you want my advice, or not?"

"I—Hassan, I haven't seen her in years. What are you talking about?" Incredulous laughter lurked beneath his words, but the smile on his face felt forced. Plastic.

"It's rather simple," Hassan said, sounding bored. "You met her. You fell in love with her. You never saw her again. You never fell out of love."

"I was fifteen." Samir meant to sound playful, but the words were unusually serious. He picked up a stray pen and spun it irritably between his fingers. "Children don't fall in love, Hassan. I liked her. I like her now. But you're being ridiculous."

"That's the silliest thing you've ever said. Of course children fall in love."

"Whatever," Samir snapped. "The point is irrelevant." Then the sound of his own impatient words hit him, and he dropped the pen. Fuck. He didn't talk to people like that. He didn't dismiss people, and he didn't lose his temper.

Especially not with his brother.

Clearing his throat, he said, "Sorry. I'm sorry. God, you're winding me up, aren't you?"

"No," Hassan said. "I'm very serious."

Samir wondered absently how much it might cost to book a flight to the Falklands and throttle his own twin.

Then his brother continued. "You knew her for six weeks and in that time you grew almost as close to her as you were to me."

"That's not tr—"

"She was your first girlfriend *and* your first love."

"She wasn't my girl—"

"When she left, you started acting more like me than like yourself, and when you realised you'd probably never see her again you didn't speak for weeks."

"I didn't speak because our parents sent me off to a fucking academic prison, and because *you* weren't there! It had nothing to do with her!"

"Nothing?" Hassan asked softly. "Do you really believe that?"

Samir's tongue felt less like a muscle and more like a wedge of sawdust filling up his throat. He tried to remember how he'd felt, in those impossible weeks after Laura left, when his life had been turned upside down. Tried, and failed. All his mind spat out was a pile of generic teenage angst with a healthy dose of fear, separation anxiety, and, of course, pure rage. Rage bright enough to burn his parents alive.

Which was normal, of course. *Nothing to see here.*

Sighing, he ran a tired hand over his face. It did little to shove those remembered, exhausting emotions back into their box. "I get what you're saying, Hassan, and maybe you're right. I mean, I know... I know that Laura and I were very close." *I know I thought I loved her, and I know she was my first and I know, I know, I know...* "But things have changed now. Honestly, how did we even get onto this topic? All I said was that she's in town!" He forced out a creaking laugh. "No-one would ever believe how dramatic you are."

"I'm not dramatic," Hassan said flatly. "I'm a romantic."

Samir blinked. "I beg your pardon?"

"That's what Joey says."

A genuine smile tugged Samir's lips at the thought of his brother's husband. He could almost imagine the words coming out of Joey's smart mouth. "I bet. Well, Mr. Romantic, you're mistaken here. There is no romance on my horizon. For one thing, Laura's pregnant."

"Interesting," Hassan said.

Samir arched a brow. "Is it? I believe it's quite a common condition."

"Oh, yes. But I suggest that you're in love with her, and your strongest evidence to the contrary is the fact that she's pregnant. Which has nothing to do with you, or with your feelings. That's what's interesting, Samir."

"Hassan. You are making me tired. You are giving me a headache."

His brother's voice was painfully smug. "For once, *I* get to irritate *you*? Excellent. How long is Laura staying?"

SHE WASN'T STALKING Samir or anything. At least, that's what Laura told herself, firmly and repeatedly, over the next few days. It was the omelettes, that was all. They were luring her in. The first one had been so good, and he'd refused to let her pay. Wasn't that how drug dealing worked?

It wasn't *her* fault that he'd gotten her addicted to omelettes.

It also wasn't her fault when she kind of, sort of, accidentally wound up at Bianchi's every day that week.

The upside of spending so much time there, aside from the omelettes, was that Samir started sitting with her on his breaks. So they got to talk about things like what her sister Hayley was up to—not much, to Laura's ever-lasting concern—and the recipes he was considering introducing to the menu.

"Even though I think you're wrong," he'd added. "No-one around here really wants Italian food."

"They would if Max made it," she sighed wistfully.

"Oh, so you think he's a better cook than I am?"

"No comment."

Sometime during the week, the locals decided it was safe

to start chatting with her. Maybe because she obviously knew Samir; maybe because Kelly and Daisy started talking to her too, asking questions about the baby and sharing pictures of Kelly and Max's younger kids. Or maybe because Max himself actually ventured out of the kitchen one day to see her, which was apparently an unheard-of occurrence.

"Just wanted to meet Samir's mysterious visitor," he'd said, smiling down from a truly unbelievable height. He was thin as a whippet, with warm brown skin and a manner so self-assured, it was almost... soothing? She could see why he and Samir were so close. She could also see why Max thought she was Samir's 'visitor'; she seemed to spend all her time at Bianchi's.

It wasn't that she'd come here looking for him—she really hadn't. She'd never thought she'd see him again. But that was a whole different story.

She'd come here looking for peace. Happiness. The sense of belonging and tranquility that she'd only ever felt once before, for six precious weeks, in this little seaside town. And if she felt that most strongly when she happened to be at Bianchi's—if she seemed like a calmer, purer, better version of herself when she was trading laughing barbs with Samir—well, that couldn't be helped, now could it?

When Max put vinegar all over her omelette because Samir told him that's how she liked it, or when Daisy made her a perfect decaf cappuccino without asking, or when Kelly spent her breaks telling Laura about breathing techniques and cocoa butter… Laura felt like she might actually be able to do this, no matter what her sister said, what her mother said, what Daniel said. And that was a gift.

But honestly? The best part of her day happened when

night fell and the moon rose, and she met Samir on the beach.

CHAPTER FIVE

A WEEK after Laura had arrived in Beesley, the moon wasn't full anymore.

But it still shone bright, and the night was clear enough that when she approached, Samir saw her coming. He *watched* her coming, in fact, and tried not to enjoy it too much.

Unfortunately, he failed.

The wind whipped her hair in wild swirls until she looked like some kind of goddess. Like a siren. He remembered the way she used to be when she hit the water, the way she'd transform in the ocean, and wondered if she still swam.

She must. Everyone had a passion they couldn't choose to leave behind, and swimming was hers.

She sat beside him awkwardly, holding her little belly as she sank onto the sand. He resisted the urge to help her because she got all huffy whenever he tried. Honestly, it was a miracle she let him do anything for her at all. He had a strong suspicion that she only came into the cafe for regular omelettes. He was starting to wish that she'd come in just to see him.

But the omelette thing was good too. After all, he hadn't been joking about looking after her. His ridiculous brother was right about one thing: this woman had once been a girl who'd lit up his universe. The least he could do was pick up the slack left by every shitty human being who'd let her come out here to do this all alone.

"Every time we meet on the beach," he admitted, "I have this urge to say something dramatic."

She smiled, moonlight glancing off her plump cheeks. "Such as?"

"You know. *We meet again.* Something like that."

"Ah, Bianchi," she murmured gravely. "I should've known I'd find you here."

He couldn't help his laughter. "Yes! Like that. Exactly like that."

She gave a little bow, hair spilling over her shoulders. "Please, hold the applause."

Something about the familiarity of the moment—the easy belonging, the casual happiness—sank into his bones. It settled there, making him feel whole and anchored in a way he hadn't for years. Here it was again, that thunderclap feeling of *You're for me, aren't you?* no less intense in adulthood than it had been during his teens. Beneath that lay a tingling undercurrent of something indescribable. It was powerful as a riptide, and just as dangerous.

Just as exhilarating, too.

But he wouldn't let himself be dragged under. He

couldn't take care of Laura while he was lusting after her, so he simply wouldn't lust.

Easy.

She stretched out beside him on the sand, leaning back on her elbows, staring up at the starry sky. And then, after a moment, she said it. "What happened?"

He'd kind of been waiting for this, and kind of dreading it, too. "When I stopped calling, you mean?"

"Yeah." There was no judgement in her voice, no accusation or even disappointment—but why would there be? They were adults now. The stormy emotions of back then were so far removed from who they were today. Even if, at that moment, Samir didn't feel removed at all.

He'd spent so long wondering if she'd hate him, or if she'd understand. If she'd believe whatever his parents fed her, or if she'd realise that their poisonous tongues were incapable of truth. Sometimes he'd wondered if she'd even care. If she'd notice when he disappeared.

Apparently, she'd noticed. That thought shouldn't cradle his heart so gently, should it?

"It was silly," he said, his voice heavy. He was already tired, and he hadn't even told her the story. "I fucked up, and it was so ridiculous. The pettiest bullshit ever."

She waited patiently while he collected his thoughts, reining in the echoes of that long-ago anger and frustration. When he spoke again, he was secure in the knowledge that Laura would most definitely listen. She'd listen like no-one else could.

Maybe that was why he'd never really told anyone else. Maybe he'd been waiting to tell her.

"So I wanted some cereal," he began, and then he had to

pause, just to laugh. How could a story like this start with such an innocuous phrase? *I wanted some cereal. I wanted some cereal, and then my life fell apart.* "I went to the kitchen, made the cereal, ate it by the sink. Washed up, put everything away. You know how they were."

He saw her nodding in the low light. Then she made a soft, encouraging sort of noise—the kind that said she was right there with him, but she didn't want to interrupt. See, she always knew exactly what to do. She always got things just right, at least as far as he was concerned. He used to get things just right with her, too, but now she seemed so different, he wondered if he'd ever learn her again.

Well, he probably wouldn't have time to. She was here to have a baby. So she'd have it.

And then she'd leave.

"About an hour later," he went on, "there was this racket from the kitchen—shouting, plates smashing, all that shit. So I ran in because I thought maybe Hassan... I don't know. I thought he was in trouble, and I wanted to help. But he wasn't there. It was Dad throwing the plates, and Ma was standing there watching him with that *look* she used to have..." He narrowed his eyes, because he couldn't describe it so much as he could reflect it. He'd grown up with that look. The look that meant she was about to slice him open on that tongue of hers, just to watch him bleed. And then throw him to his father's big bad wolf.

"Dad was flipping out because I didn't clean up after myself. I left the milk out, the cereal out, mess all over the counter, dirty bowl by the sink. But I didn't. Obviously, I didn't, because Jesus, I'd never be so fucking stupid. I swore it wasn't me, so he called Hassan in. And Hassan, of course, swore it wasn't him.

"But it *was*. I knew it was. It had to be, because it wasn't me. And that meant he'd not only done something that would drop us both in the shit, he was trying to pin it on me. I couldn't believe it. And they believed him, they took his side, and I was so fucking furious, and he was acting furious too, like I'd really done something, and I couldn't believe his fucking nerve so I—I hit him. I hit my brother." He ran a hand over his face as he breathed through the memory. That was the part he still couldn't get over, the part that brought bile to his throat no matter how many years passed—the feel of his brother's nose breaking beneath his fist, bone and cartilage crunching, blood spilling out.

He'd thrown up right after. And when it was all over, his dad had made him clean up the vomit.

Samir cleared his throat, pushing past the regret that clogged it. "Well, the second I did it, it was like a spell broke or something. I realised straight away—of course it wasn't Hassan. Of course he wouldn't lie. He wouldn't fuck me over just to protect himself. It couldn't be him. That's when I realised it was my mother." He laughed, but the sound was forced. "You know how she was. My parents liked to fuck with each other's heads. Ma liked to fuck with ours. To try and turn us against each other. One minute you're looking for someone's lost keys, the next she's convinced you that you ate the fucking keys and now you're losing your mind. I don't know why I fell for it, even for a second. Usually when she pulled stuff like that, I just kept my mouth shut and took the punishment but…"

37

But it'd been a week since Laura and her family had left, since her holiday had ended, and she'd disappeared from his life beyond snatched phone conversations. So he hadn't been thinking straight, and he'd wanted to argue, wanted to fight.

Just like his parents.

"When I realised it was her, I… lost it. I started screaming, throwing shit at her, throwing shit at Dad, and I told them they were both crazy bastards and I was reporting them to fucking Childline or something." He gave a bitter laugh. "I don't know. I was pissed. They were pissed too, I guess. What'd they tell you, when you called?"

"They… they said you'd gone to boarding school," Laura murmured. "They told me not to call. Because you weren't coming back."

"I suppose that's right, really. I went to a boarding school for kids with behavioural and emotional issues, to deal with my 'explosive anger problem.'" He rolled his eyes. "It… it wasn't fun. I heard those schools are a hell of a lot better now, but then… it wasn't fun." He shrugged. "They didn't send Hassan, either. They separated us. That part was almost easier, though, because I didn't have to worry about him anymore, and he didn't have to worry about me. We could survive on our own."

He wasn't surprised at her silence. It was probably a lot to take in. But he was surprised that, when she finally spoke, it was to ask, "So who broke your nose?"

"Hassan," he said. "Hassan did it."

"And you let him, didn't you?"

"Well… yeah. I broke his."

Out of nowhere, he felt the brush of her hand over his in

the dark. The first time she'd touched him since they'd met again. It shot through him with the force of a tidal wave.

She laced her fingers through his, slowly, methodically, as if it was important that they do this completely and successfully. Once she had him, their palms locked together, that single point of contact anchoring him, she lapsed into silence again.

And he was content.

CHAPTER SIX

"You okay locking up?"

"Stop asking." Max rolled his eyes, slicing mushrooms without even looking. The sight would never not worry Samir. He had very few friends, and the last thing he wanted was for one of them to chop their own finger off.

But if Max hadn't dismembered himself yet, he probably never would.

"Cool." Samir put the keys beside Max's chopping board and clapped him *gently* on the back. Wouldn't want to nudge that rapidly-slicing knife. He had plans that didn't include taking Max to A&E, and he'd hate to leave his best mate bleeding tragically all over the kitchen. "See you tomorrow."

"See you," Max said, his voice far too innocent. "Good luck."

Samir scowled. "What? I—why are you wishing *me*—wait, no, never mind. Doesn't matter. You're just trying to wind me up."

Max's answering laughter followed him out of the kitchen.

It had been almost four weeks since Laura had arrived in Beesley. Three weeks since he'd started taking his lunch break at her table—which was categorically *not* a date, since he was at work and she was just his friend. His friend whose presence, whose smile, whose growing trust in him, felt as fresh and untouchable as sea foam.

Platonic sea foam, obviously. As opposed to adoring, lustful sea foam, which Samir knew absolutely nothing about.

Two weeks since he'd offered to drive her to the hospital for her 20-week scan—you know, since she'd never been to their local hospital before. Norfolk was a treacherous place, what with all the aggressive good cheer and suspiciously polite old folks. She could get lost, or be kidnapped by a band of holidaying children. These things happened.

One week since she, after six straight days of blushing and lip-biting and squinting and *Ummms*, had said yes.

And it would probably take several hundred years for his best friend to stop teasing him about the whole thing.

He couldn't pretend he minded, though. Samir hadn't had many friends as a kid—it wasn't easy to bond with people when he was busy trying to survive his parents' reign of emotional terror. So the good-natured mockery was... nice. He just didn't want Laura to hear the guys in the kitchen calling him *Dad* or asking him about the baby, because she'd probably overthink it and die of embarrassment.

She met him outside, even though she'd been sitting in the cafe five minutes ago. She hadn't said it, but he got the impression that she didn't want the townspeople to think they were together in any way. Which they obviously weren't.

A couple of weeks ago, he'd overheard one of the town's unrepentantly nosy old women ask Laura, "Are you *married, dear?*" As if it wasn't pretty clear, by this point, that she wasn't married. Laura had glanced at her own bare ring finger before saying, "I'm divorced." Her voice had been strange. Off. As if she was lying. So now he had this suspicion that she'd never been married at all, but she didn't want people to know. And he wanted to tell her that it really didn't matter, but she hadn't told *him*, so acting like he knew would be rude, wouldn't it?

"Hey," she said, her voice snatching him out of his thoughts. "You ready?"

"Yeah. Sorry." He opened the car door for her, and she smiled. It was a small smile, contained, and she lowered her gaze as she slid into the car. There must be something wrong with him, because he snatched up that hint of pleasure like a dog taking crumbs from the table.

Ah, well. If he had to be pathetic over someone, it might as well be someone as beautiful as Laura.

He got into the driver's seat and said, "My car sucks."

"Does it? I wouldn't know."

"I thought you might be a car girl. You know, cuz you drive that monster." He pulled out onto the main road, feeling like he'd never driven before. Laura was in his car—in his *care*—which meant he sure as shit better look both ways.

"Oh, it's not mine. It's my—it's Bump's grandpa's." She put a hand to her stomach. She'd been doing that a lot more, these past weeks, maybe because she'd suddenly gotten a hell of a lot bigger. And, of course, she'd started calling the baby *Bump*. All of these things, independently, were adorable, but put them together and Samir frequently struggled not to melt in her presence.

Right now, though, what caught his attention was the guarded edge in her voice. It didn't sound like she wanted to pursue the *Bump's grandpa* thing, even if the words—and her slight hesitation—had piqued his curiosity. He was always curious where Laura was concerned. He felt like a bloodhound, sometimes, picking up every scent, hunting down all the little things she didn't say.

But he wouldn't push her. He knew that she loved to swim, and that she was kind of anal about her hair. He knew she'd studied Politics and IR, and that she loved profiteroles more than life itself. He didn't need all of her secrets when he knew how to make her smile, did he? Friends didn't tell each other everything.

So instead of asking about Bump's grandpa, he said, "Speaking of Bump. You have any name ideas?"

"Of course I do!"

"You do?"

"Oh, yeah. The problem is..." She trailed off, but he could almost feel her laughter, bubbling beneath the surface. "The problem is, my ideas are awful."

He raised a brow. "You think of names you don't like?"

"Oh, no, I like them. It's just... Okay, so I have this friend—well, I don't know. We weren't friends at all, which was my fault. I was kind of awful to her, actually." The cheer in her voice had evaporated into empty nothingness. He didn't like that. He wanted the happiness back.

So he said, "But you're friends now?"

"Well, yes. I think so. You can never be too sure with Ruth. We're friendly, at least. I like her a lot." And then, as if she couldn't hold back the words: "She's my ex's ex. So we... we started having coffee. We had stuff to talk about."

Stuff to talk about? That sounded ominous.

"Anyway!" Laura said, and her voice was too light all of a sudden, all *let's-move-past-that-part-shall-we?*

So he said, "Yeah, anyway. Ruth?"

"Well, she's very honest. *Painfully* honest. She would never lie. So I've been asking her opinion on my names, and she had... feedback. Strong feedback."

Even though Laura sounded amused rather than upset, Samir felt a flare of indignation. "Well, what does she know? Maybe she's wrong. You need more than one opinion."

"I chose her as a sounding board because she's so sensible. I do realise that my choices can get a bit... flamboyant."

"What are your choices? And what's she been saying?"

Laura snorted. "Hang on, I'll read you the texts." She shuffled around in her seat, because her little bag had somehow gotten caught behind her. Her breasts bounced with every wiggling movement, but Samir didn't watch because he was a gentleman, and gentlemen did not ogle unsuspecting friends—even if said friends happened to be unreasonably hot.

Laura finally reached her bag, produced her phone, and began reading out texts with wry intonation. "Okay, here we go. Me: 'How about Canon?' Ruth—"

Samir nearly crashed the car. "Did you just say *Canon?*"

"Yes," Laura replied calmly. "It's badass. And gender-neutral."

He stared at her as best he could while keeping an eye on the road.

"What?" she demanded.

"I'm just trying to figure out," he mused, "how you could seem like such a reasonable human being, but secretly harbour a desire to name your innocent baby *Canon*."

"You and Ruth would get on so well."

"What did she say?"

"As I was going to tell you before I was so *rudely* interrupted—"

"If you expected me to contain myself at *Canon*, you really don't know me at all."

She raised her voice over his mutterings. "Ruth said: 'Do you want your baby to suffer?'"

"I've changed my mind about Ruth. You're right. She should have final say on all baby names."

Laura snorted. "Not *final* say—"

"Final say."

"You haven't heard my other ideas yet!"

"Okay," he said mildly. "You have three chances to convince me that you're capable of naming this baby."

"Who died and made you the baby king?"

"Your good judgement."

She laughed, and the sound washed over him like spring rain. "Alright, um… Let me think of the best ones… Okay, so, Satyr."

"No."

"Ocean."

"Laura," he said, very seriously. "Are you trying to kill me?"

"Oh my God, shut up. I like the ocean! The ocean is

mighty! It's beautiful! And I'll be living right by it through this pregnancy, so it's… symbolic, and stuff."

"Last chance. Third name."

She huffed. "You're very closed-minded."

"I'm trying to save your child from a lifetime of terrible jokes."

"Fine. What about Solo?"

Samir felt a migraine coming on. "As in… Han Solo?"

"No!" she said, clearly outraged. "As in Solange!"

"Solange…?"

There was a pause. Then she gave a pained sort of sigh. "I'm going to pretend you didn't just say that."

"Okay." He felt his lips twitch. "But here's an idea—why don't you just call the kid Solange?"

"Because I don't know Bump's gender! So it has to be *neutral*. Okay?" She peered at him suspiciously, as if he might be deliberately sabotaging her cursed baby name campaign.

Samir cleared his throat and did his best to sound serious. "Alright, I get it. So you want something like… Willow?"

"Hm." She pursed her lips. He awaited her verdict with baited breath. Or rather, he held his breath to stop himself from chuckling at her adorably grave expression. Finally, she admitted, "I quite like that."

"Really?"

"Well, it's okay. A bit plain, though."

He didn't bother to hold back his laughter, now. "Oh, Laura. What am I going to do with you?"

"I imagine that's up to you," she said. And something in her voice caught him, hooked him, had his fingers tightening around the steering wheel and his gaze darting toward her. But she was looking out of the window, the curtain of her hair hiding her face.

He'd probably been imagining things, anyway.

LAURA'S BELLY looked like an iced bun. An iced bun with raspberry jam dribbling down the sides. She really hadn't expected to get stretch marks so suddenly.

She'd always been rather fond of raspberry jam.

"Ready? It's cold." The grim-faced sonographer didn't wait for a response before slapping icy jelly all over Laura's midriff.

"Crikey," Laura muttered. "You weren't joking."

"Mmm," the woman grunted. She was relatively young, red-headed, and apparently in a bad mood. Or perhaps she was just a grunting sort of woman.

Daniel had red hair. Would Bump have red hair? Probably not. It was a recessive gene or something.

Laura waited in self-conscious silence for something interesting to happen on the screen to her right. It felt odd doing this alone. The last scan she'd had, her sister had been right there with her, and they'd cooed at the blurry image as if it looked like a baby instead of a staticky kidney bean. For those precious minutes, she and Hayley had actually managed to get on.

Now Hayley was miles away and pissed at her—as usual —and Laura didn't have anyone to squeal with. Well, she supposed that wasn't entirely true: she could've squealed with Samir. He'd asked, right before she'd gotten out of the car. "Hey, Laura, you don't—I mean, are you okay going in on your own? Because I don't mind—"

"It's fine," she'd said, bright as the sunshine. Totally, utterly, 100% okay, that was her! She had to make it completely believable, you see—*beyond* believable—because she'd had this sick feeling that Samir might insist, if he thought she wanted company. And while part of her thought it might be nice to have him along, her rational brain knew that was just the crush talking.

Yes, she had a crush on Samir. He was Samir, for Christ's sake.

Which was exactly why she hadn't let him come in. It was one thing for a *friend*-friend to help out, but an inconveniently-sexy-friend who inspired weird, flushed feelings was a different matter entirely.

And yet, she'd let him drive her here. She'd even perved over his forearms during the journey. Oh dear. She was a shameless, crush-stricken hussy. A... crushy. If she didn't watch herself, all these inconvenient feelings might bubble over like pasta left on the stove, and then where would she be? Lost and glum and lustful, with her knickers in a twist. That's where.

So, no, she decided, she did *not* want to squeal with Samir. Even if her heart did backflips every time he smiled at her. Even if it was almost painfully sweet of him to offer.

And yet... when she imagined someone sitting beside her during this moment, it wasn't Hayley, or her father-in-law, Trevor, or even Ruth.

It was him.

"Five more minutes and we're done," the sonographer said. "Everything looks just fine."

"Wonderful!" Laura said brightly. Probably too brightly, if the sonographer's obvious alarm was anything to go by. *Oops.*

"You've got a big one," the woman added, "but you probably knew that already."

Well, Laura was a big person. Daniel was a big person. She'd kind of assumed.

"Just you today?" the sonographer's assistant asked. Apparently, she felt like breaking the ice.

"Yep," Laura said. *Just me every day.* She looked down at her iced bun of a belly and felt some of her earlier satisfaction fading. Daniel had said she'd ruin her body. He'd reminded her how vain she was.

He didn't seem to realise that her obsession with her appearance had more to do with him than it did with her.

But he was out of her life now, wasn't he? So his opinion didn't matter anymore. And Laura's belly looked delicious, she decided. Why, you could probably sell it at a patisserie. Except not really, because if anyone tried to eat her baby, she'd yank their brains out through their nostrils. That would probably reduce customer satisfaction quite significantly.

The scan took less than half an hour altogether, and the baby was pronounced healthy. When Laura came outside, the air felt warmer than she remembered. Samir wasn't waiting in the car; he was leaning against it, arms folded, his eyes trained on the hospital's entrance. When he saw her, he straightened up with a smile. And when he saw the little paper pouch in her hands, his grin widened.

"You got pictures?"

"Yes," she said. That was all she could say. She was

utterly disarmed by how excited he seemed to be. He was bouncing slightly on his heels like a kid waiting for dessert. Was this normal? Perhaps he was having a funny turn.

"Can I see?" he asked. No funny turns, then; he really was *that* excited about a horrendously poor-quality photo.

"Of course." She gave him the folder. He slid the photograph out and stared at the blurry, blobby, black-and-yellow image like it was a Rembrandt.

"Would you look at that," he murmured, his gaze running over every unidentifiable shape. "Hi, Bump!"

Her heart practically burst in her chest.

CHAPTER SEVEN

THE NAMES LAURA texted him over the next two weeks were so outrageous that Samir became convinced she was trying to kill him. Of course, if she *did* have murderous intent, she could just poison him when they had lunch together—which was almost every day. Or maybe shove him into the ocean when they met on the beach—which was every single night.

On second thought, whatever she was trying to do, it probably didn't involve his eventual demise. But sometimes, when she smiled at him in a certain way, or said his name with that aching, unexplainable softness in her voice, Samir thought he might just die anyway.

When she called him on a Saturday evening in May, he hadn't seen her all day, which was a rarity. Combine that with the fact that she'd never actually *called* him before, and Samir almost had a heart attack when her name flashed up on his caller ID. He brought the phone to his ear so hard and so fast, he wouldn't be surprised if he'd bruised his own bloody face. "Laura? Are you okay? What's going on?"

"Well, hello to you too," she said, and that was all it took for him to relax. She was fine. He could hear it the way he heard her sadness sometimes, or her nerves, or her whirring, worrying mind.

Samir sank back in his office chair and smiled. At this point, it was an automatic response to the sound of her voice. "You called. You never call."

"That's funny. Bump's grandpa said the same thing this afternoon."

"Oh?" Samir didn't need to know anything about this mysterious grandparent. Even so, he froze, every atom of his body at attention, just in case she was about to say…. *something*. Something that would reveal more of her secrets to him. Something that might explain the shadows he saw in her, the ones he couldn't quite shine a light on.

But in the end, all he got was an absent, "Mmm. Anyway, I was actually…" She trailed off for a moment, sounding almost painfully self-conscious, the way she did sometimes. She'd never been like that before. It was funny; adulthood and freedom from his parents had given Samir a confidence his teenage self had only ever faked. But something in Laura's life had done the opposite to her, unravelling the once-tight threads of her self-esteem. He wanted to know what.

Though he already had some ideas.

She cleared her throat, and he could almost see her now: lifting her chin, setting those broad shoulders like a general. He liked that, liked those moments when she paused and pulled herself together; those moments when she made a conscious decision to be brave.

He wondered what she was being brave about this time.

Then she told him outright. "I was wondering if you'd like to come over for dinner."

He almost fell out of his chair. "Dinner?" Shit. Had his voice always been so rough?

"Yes. I have all these prawns that need to be eaten," she said, her tone almost defiantly casual. "Or, you know, they'll go off. There's a lot. I lost it in Sainsbury's last week and bought a shit ton."

"Ah. So you're recruiting the greediest eater you know for assistance?"

"Yep!" she said promptly. As if there was absolutely no other reason why she'd ever ask.

He wasn't disappointed. That would be childish. His very platonic, very untouchable, highly adorable *friend* was inviting him to dinner, and there was absolutely nothing disappointing about that.

So Samir made sure to sound especially cheerful when he replied. "I'm up to the challenge. When do you want me?"

"Oh, any time. I'm hardly busy. All I do is order too much baby stuff online and reread *The Secret*."

He snorted. "In that case, I'd better come and save you from yourself."

"Right now?"

"Right now."

"Lovely," she said. "I'll leave the door unlocked."

~

LAURA MADE dinner in this long, low-slung skirt that floated when she moved. There was a little gap between the hem of her T-shirt and the waistband of that skirt, and when she reached up to get ingredients out of the cupboard, that gap widened. Then she'd lower her arms, and the gap would narrow again.

Slowly, steadily, the skin revealed and concealed by that gap sent Samir out of his fucking mind. By the time she produced dessert, his conversation was reduced to babbled inanities like, "Oh. Jelly. Did you make this?"

"Is it that obvious? I've been making tons of sweets recently. Cravings." She grimaced and scooped up a spoonful. The silver slid between her lips a little too slowly for Samir's peace of mind, her fine mouth plumping under the pressure. Then she released the spoon with a pop that shot straight to his dick. *Shit.* "I think it's quite good," she said thoughtfully. "Maybe the best batch yet."

He rammed a chunk of jelly into his gob to stop himself saying something reckless. Something like, *It looks great, but I'd rather eat you.*

He definitely, *definitely* couldn't say that.

Bright, tropical flavour burst across his tongue as the jelly slid down his throat. Jesus. Samir took another spoonful, his inappropriate lust almost forgotten. Such was the power of a damned good dessert.

"That's amazing," he spluttered.

That familiar, raspberry flush crept up her throat. "Thanks," she said, sounding almost shy. "Jelly's my thing right now. I used to hate it, actually. My taste buds have gone all weird." She rested her free hand absently on the swell of her belly, just beneath her breasts. Not that he noticed her breasts. Except for the fact that they seemed bigger every time he saw her. Because she was pregnant. Babies! He'd think about babies. That would help.

He managed to hold a half-decent conversation through dessert by turning the topic to Bump, and Laura's next scan, and some weird woman on Mumsnet who claimed that anyone using disposable nappies was cursing their child's very existence from the start. Convincing Laura that, no, she did *not* have to use fabric nappies just because some stranger online said so, was surprisingly difficult.

"I told Trevor about it," she said, and then added, as if it were an afterthought, "That's Bump's grandpa. Trevor."

Samir filed the information away in his sadly slim folder of *Things I Know About Laura's Life.*

"I told him," she continued, "and he said it sounded very sensible."

"Fabric nappies?" Samir said, incredulous. "Sensible? I'm guessing he's not the one who'll be washing them."

She laughed. "No. He's lovely, but sometimes he's so... old and rich and, you know." She rolled her eyes.

"Pretentious?"

"Oh, I wouldn't call Trevor pretentious. Now, *Daniel,* God, he's—" She broke off all at once, as if someone had snipped her words short with a pair of scissors. Her eyes widened, and her lips pressed together so hard they turned white.

In the next second, she was standing, snatching up both their plates.

"Are you done?" she asked brightly, even though she'd already whipped away his food.

"Uh, actually—"

"Great! If you liked the jelly, there's more. I can put it in a tub for you to take home."

Samir didn't typically respond well to food theft, but he decided to contain his instinctual outrage. And not just because she was sending him home with a box—though that certainly helped. He leant back in his seat and studied the stiff column of her spine as she moved to the sink. "Daniel, hm?"

"Sorry?" She looked over her shoulder, dark hair hanging rather conveniently across her face.

"Is that his name?"

There was a moment, a heartbeat, of tension before she said softly, "Yes."

Then she turned back to the sink and twisted on the taps, and Samir stood up, his attention quite thoroughly diverted. If she was trying to distract him, she'd chosen the right tactic.

"What on earth are you doing?" he demanded. "Sit down, woman."

She snorted out a laugh. "Don't tell me what to do."

"Fine. I strongly *suggest* that you sit down. Let me wash up." He nudged her out of the way, his shoulders butting against hers. "You cooked."

"You're a guest," she said, in that stiff little voice he remembered her mother using. Or at least, the one she'd used early in the mornings, when she wasn't piss-herself-drunk yet.

"Don't be ridiculous." He tugged the washing up liquid from her hands. "I'm just me. Anyway, I know your back hurts."

"How could you possibly know that my back hurts?"

How could he not, when he watched her constantly, when he noticed the pattern of her fucking breaths, when sometimes he felt like he could hear her heart beating?

But all he said was, "You're pregnant. Therefore, your back hurts."

"Amazing," she said dryly. "You're like my own personal midwife. So sage. So wise." But she still went to sit down, her lips curving into a reluctant smile.

And then the smile disappeared as she gasped, one hand braced against the table, the other flying to her belly.

"Laura?" Concern gripped him. He dropped the dishes, crossed the tiled floor in seconds and took her face in his hands. "What? What's—?"

She was smiling. Why was she smiling?

Without a word, she caught one of his hands and dragged it down to her stomach. His brain was still stuck in panic mode, so he didn't even realise what it meant when she pressed his palm flat against her bump.

Then he felt what she'd felt, and the flood of understanding almost dragged him under.

Samir held his breath as he felt an insistent little push beneath his hand—beneath Laura's *skin*. His heart stuttered in his chest, fluttering like the wings of a caged bird. Common sense flew out the window; he was all giddy excitement now. He didn't even hesitate to slide his other arm around Laura's back, to hold her in place as he spread his hand wide over her belly and felt every kick.

"Oh my God," he breathed. When he looked up, he found her grin impossibly wide and her eyes shimmering like silver ocean. "Oh my God," he said again. "That's so fucking…"

"It's weird, right?" She laughed, but it was kind of wobbly. "The weirdest thing ever!"

"It's the best, weirdest thing I've ever felt," he admitted. "Oh, angel, don't cry. Please don't cry."

"No, no, I'm fine!" Tears streamed down her cheeks, splotches of pink blooming across her face like roses. "I don't know why I'm crying! It's just so…" Samir resisted the urge to wince as her voice soared to dolphin pitch. He could hear the sounds and everything, but it kind of came out like "SoohmagahaBABYbumpallkickinrealinsideohgahisohappy!"

"That's great love," he murmured. He was rubbing her belly in circles now, which she didn't seem to mind. In fact, she wiped roughly at her face with both hands and gave him a smile brighter than the sun.

"Sorry," she sniffed. "That's just the first time I felt any kicks or anything, and I was starting to think it would never happen! And now, you know… it's happening! Oh, I got carried away. Sorry. Sorry!"

"Don't be sorry," he said, and hoped he sounded calm. Cool. Not at all like he was exploding inside over the fact that *he'd* just felt the baby's first kicks—that she'd wanted him to. He was the only person around, after all. Of course she'd wanted to share it with someone.

But now the baby seemed to have abruptly settled down, and Laura wasn't stepping away—even though his fingers brushed against that slice of bare skin with every slow circle he made. Maybe *he* should pull back. Maybe she was feeling awkward or uncomfortable and didn't know how to say 'Please get the fuck off me' politely. That was probably it.

Samir was about to let go when she looked up at him, and just like that, he felt it. That electrical charge, like the air before a storm, that coalesced between them when he least expected it. Her fingers brushed his wrist, hesitant and barely there. Then the touch came again, firmer now, until her hand was pressed over his. As if she were keeping him in place. As if she didn't want him to stop.

She definitely didn't want him to stop.

"Laura," he murmured. "Tell me... tell me what you're thinking."

Her smile fading, she ran her tongue over her lower lip. It was a nervous gesture, he told himself. That was all. Just because her eyes were starlight and her cheeks were flushed and he could see the rise and fall of her chest getting faster and heavier, didn't mean he should assume anything.

Then she said, "I'm wondering why you still make me feel like this."

"Like what?"

She spoke so softly, he barely heard her. "Perfect."

Samir's eyes slid shut as if blocking out the sight of her could block out everything else. As if he could ignore his inconvenient adoration, or the surge of anticipation flooding his veins. He had to be careful. This could all go dangerously wrong. *He* could be dangerously wrong, to hear that word and think it meant she wanted him. 'Perfect' could mean anything. The low, husky tone of her voice could mean anything.

Her hand sliding up his arm, his shoulder, sinking into his hair—that could mean anything.

Couldn't it?

He opened his eyes and found her, still real, still standing there in his arms, but unimaginably changed. That ever-cool gaze was heated mercury, burning into him the way it used to. The way he shouldn't even remember. When he thought of her, on the nights when he was too tired or too reckless or too fucking besotted to stop himself, she looked at him just like this.

"Say something," he gritted out.

"Like what?"

"I don't know. *Don't. Stop. No—*"

She pressed her hand over his mouth, cutting off his words, his thoughts, his good sense. Then her palm slid away until only the tips of her fingers grazed his lips. She leaned close, so fucking close, and suddenly he could feel her against him, from the lush jut of her breasts to the firm press of her belly. Her lips hovered over her fingers, which hovered over *his* lips... And oh, Christ, he was so fucking gone. Cock hard as hammer and mind utterly scrambled and willpower crumbled to dust. Why would he ever want to resist her anyway? Why would he ever want to do anything other than sink into all that perfection?

He felt her breath ghost over his lips, whispering through her fingers as she murmured, "What I want to say is *yes.*"

He gulped down air as if he were in danger of drowning. "But you're afraid. I know you're afraid."

Something in her gaze faltered, which wasn't what he'd wanted. He just wanted her to be sure. Because he'd watched her—he always watched her—and he knew that she flinched when people came too close or moved too fast. He knew that she was nervous all the time—not a lot, but enough—and that she had this low thrum of constant anxiety keeping her on edge. He knew that she was always waiting, even when she seemed happiest, for the other shoe to drop.

And still, despite all that, she whispered, "I am. But I don't want to be."

CHAPTER EIGHT

LAURA KNEW, somewhere in the back of her mind, that she shouldn't be doing this. And yet, she couldn't stop. It was so deliciously alien to feel this way, so decadent, so intense, and such a fucking relief.

Yes; it was a relief when he pressed soft kisses to the tips of her fingers until her eyes slid shut. It was a relief when he pushed her hand away so gently, and let his lips glide over hers, light as his breath had been. It was a relief when he combed his fingers into her hair, just to hold her, and grasped her hips, just to touch her. Not dragging her down like an anchor, but helping her stay afloat.

He was so tentative as he tasted her. So careful as his lips, all full and hot and *him*, caressed hers with a quiet, patient intensity that warmed her from the inside out. And she remembered, all of a sudden—through faded impressions, snatches of teenage awkwardness and the frantic, reckless hearts thudding at the centre of it all—that this was how it used to be. This was the first time all over again, and it was more than just a dream.

But beyond the sweet delicacy that was so right, and so *Samir*, she felt something else, too. Something she wanted. Something humming just beneath his surface, tightly coiled and ravenous, burning through the tense column of his body, spurring on her growing desperation.

Until, finally, his tongue eased into her mouth with a sureness that lit her up like a sparkler in the dark. And something in Laura snapped.

She opened for him with a moan that revealed every filthy thought she'd ever been quietly ashamed of—only, now that he was kissing her, she couldn't be ashamed anymore. The knowledge that he wouldn't stop her, or hate her for wanting like this, let Laura lust recklessly. It let her catch his T-shirt in frantic, grasping fingers, and slide her eager hands over every inch of his skin she could reach.

He stiffened against her for a moment before everything about him went hot and liquid and hard all at once, his arms tightening around her body as if he couldn't get close enough, as if he couldn't feel enough of her. He pinned her to him like they were in some black-and-white film, and she understood the appeal of those things now, because this felt *good*. This felt like pure passion, like pinpricks of light and heat darting through her body until she was nothing but a constellation of pleasure. And all he'd done was kiss her desperately, hold her as if he couldn't let go, hear the silent pleas of her hungry mouth against his and reply in kind.

He moved, dragging her with him, and she didn't understand but let it happen anyway. Samir caught her legs, lifted them up either side of his waist, and then she felt cool wood against her knees and realised that they were sprawled over the kitchen table. She was *straddling* his *lap*. Good Lord. This was not the sort of thing people did on kitchen tables!

But apparently, it was the sort of thing Samir Bianchi did. And it was the sort of thing she did when she was with him. Oh, this was divine. Delicious. When she broke the kiss, blinking down at him in surprise, he gave her one of those wicked smiles and murmured, "Whatever you do, don't start thinking."

Which Laura thought was excellent advice.

He planted one of those big, bold hands on her arse, ran the other through her hair, and pulled her down to kiss him again. Just like that, the only thing in the world was his mouth licking and gasping against hers, and his greedy hands, and the lustful rhythm he drove through her veins. The only thing that mattered was having him. That, and being had.

She felt the rigid outline of his erection beneath her, so she rolled her hips and shifted and fidgeted while he groaned—"Fuck, Laura, what are you...?"—until she found the perfect position. *There.* That thick, stiff pressure was flush against her aching pussy, her skirt gathered around her knees, his jeans rough against her underwear. Perfect. *Perfect.*

She rocked her swollen clit against his hardness and Samir hissed, hips jerking. "That's it, angel," he rasped, his eyes impossibly dark, inescapably hungry. "You look so beautiful, Laura. So beautiful right now, rubbing yourself all over my cock, blushing for me..." He ran one of those calloused palms over her throat, her chest, touching her as if he couldn't stop. Then his hand moved lower, sliding beneath the neckline of her dress, cupping her aching breast. She released a jagged cry, and he smiled, too slow and fucking sexy to bear. "Sensitive, love?"

"Yes," she gasped.

"Too much?"

"No, no, no, keep, *fuck*—"

"You are *so* turned on," he murmured, almost talking to himself. He bit his lip as he kneaded her aching breast, just on the edge of roughness. "I want to keep you like this. Forever. Always."

"Ohhh, God," she moaned, her hips working faster, her breaths coming out in frantic whimpers, something impossibly hot and right and good swelling inside her.

"Why'd you have to be so fucking beautiful?" He sounded so genuinely put out, his voice hoarse and hopeless, that she almost laughed. But then his other hand—fuck, those hands were never still—snaked beneath the fabric of her skirt, and oh, she wasn't laughing anymore.

He pushed her hips away from the delicious pressure of his dick, and she released a low, desperate whine. Then he kissed her hard and fast, a gunshot claiming of the lips, an electric thrust of his tongue against hers. "Shh," he soothed, and she felt his palm, firm and hot over her pussy, searing through the fabric of her underwear. He pushed the heel of his hand tight against her aching clit, and she whimpered. "That's better," he murmured in her ear. "Yeah? That's better, isn't it, love?" But he already knew. His middle finger eased over her mound, spreading those pouting lips through the cotton, the sensation muffled and just short of perfect.

"Oh, please, more," she gasped, rocking against him. "Touch me. I need—I need—"

Then he hooked a finger beneath the fabric of her knickers and pulled them aside. She felt cool air hit the wet heat of her pussy, and apparently, *that* was what she needed.

"Fuck," she gasped. *"Fuck."*

He slid one thick, blunt finger over her slippery flesh, circling her entrance, sending sparks through her body as if his touch contained lightning. "So fucking wet," he muttered, his cheeks dark and flushed, his eyes heavy-lidded, his voice thick and low and decadent. "Like this, angel?"

"Inside me."

"I fucking wish," he gritted out, even as he eased two fingers into her. She whimpered at the slick stretch, that delicious glide as he filled her, the sound of her own wetness making her blush. But it was hard to feel too embarrassed with the heel of his hand firm against her clit, and the thick intrusion of his fingers spreading her open just right, and his heated gaze pinned to hers.

"You know how I'd fuck you?" he murmured. "I'd fuck you from behind. You'd like that, wouldn't you?" He curved his fingers inside her, stroking her, until she moaned and sank her teeth into her lower lip. "I'd have you on your knees. On all fours. I'd spread you open with my fingers and watch my dick push deep into this hot, sweet cunt." Oh, *fuck*. She wanted that.

He rubbed against a place inside her that made stars swirl before her eyes, and then he did it again and again, until pleasure swelled through her like a sunrise. The sensation pushed her beyond that pale thing called desire to something utterly mindless, painfully hedonistic, inhumanly raw. Laura licked at the thick, amber column of his throat, just because she needed to taste him, and he groaned, the sound hoarse and broken. So she followed the need, let it rule her, sucking and licking and biting at his neck until a slight bruise bloomed beneath his skin.

"Jesus," he whispered, his expression almost pained, his fingers never faltering. "Keep doing that. Laura. *Laura.*" She licked a path up to his jaw, sucking and dragging her teeth along his stubbled skin, and his hand tightened in her hair as if he might restrain her. But he didn't. He wouldn't. She felt the weight of his touch, his contained strength, and underneath it all, his adoration.

He pushed his hips up against hers, even with his hand trapped between their bodies, as if he couldn't help it. "You're gonna make me come," he rasped out. "Laura. Stop."

She hesitated. "*Stop*, stop?"

"No," he groaned, rising up to catch her mouth with his. "No." This time, there was no gentleness, no careful, tentative kisses—but she still felt just as revered when he licked into her, wild and reckless, as she had when he'd grazed her lips softly. His tongue thrust against hers as his fingers sped up inside her, and she felt that uncontrollable fluttering as her core tightened and her breaths became gasping sobs and—

Oh. Oh oh oh *this...*

She felt everything all at once, more than should be humanly possible, and heard him whispering "I have you," and was grateful he'd said it because she felt like she was lost in an ocean of bliss that might never end. As if she'd eaten fairy fruit and was trapped in the kind of pure pleasure that simply couldn't be good for her.

But it *felt* good, *so* good, the definition of fucking good, to cry out and stiffen and collapse against him. And after a second, when her breathing slowed and her swirling pleasure stilled enough to think, she realised that she wasn't even lying down, exactly—he was holding her up, taking all of her weight so that the swell of her belly didn't have to. Fuck. She'd forgotten about that.

She'd forgotten about that.

Oh, shit. Oh, *shit.*

Laura returned to earth with a sickening *thud*, her teeth and bones jarred, her afterglow snuffed out before it had a chance to breathe.

And he knew, of course. Instantly, he knew.

"Laura?" Samir looked up with so much softness in his gaze, so much care. She recognised it. He used to look at her like that before, when neither of them had fully understood what it meant.

What the fuck had she done?

"I'm sorry," she choked out, her voice so strangled the words were barely intelligible.

But he heard. She knew he heard, because for a moment his expression was heartbreaking. Then that soul-deep sadness disappeared so fast, she might have imagined it. He frowned, an arrow forming between those sharp brows, his impossibly thick lashes sweeping down as he looked away. His eyelashes always had been ridiculous. His whole fucking face was ridiculous. He was beautiful. Maybe that was why she'd lost all her good sense. Only, really, she knew it wasn't. She knew *exactly* why her control had gone walkabout, and it wasn't because Samir was too handsome to function.

It was because, even now, in this terrible, tense moment, he had the fucking temerity to *help her up*. To help her clamber off him—off the bloody kitchen table!—as if she weren't ashamed enough. He was a wonderful, brilliant bastard, and all of a sudden, she couldn't stand him.

"I'm sorry," she repeated, on her own two feet this time. Laura pulled up the neckline of her T-shirt, and rearranged her skirt, and wondered if she could subtly slide her knickers back into place or if she'd have to leave them wonky under her clothes.

"Sorry for what?" he asked, cutting through her frantically mundane thoughts.

"For—I—I shouldn't have…" She cleared her throat. Pulled herself together. "That was a mistake. Obviously. That was a mistake. I shouldn't have done that."

"Ah," he said. Just, *Ah*.

And then he was silent. Which, of course, made her say a thousand things she shouldn't. "Samir, I can't just—I have responsibilities now. Important responsibilities. And I came here to figure out how to do this—how to be a mother—without complications. And sleeping with you, or whatever this is, it can't *go* anywhere—"

His cool gaze sharpened. "Why not?"

Why not? "Samir, I'm having a baby. I'm not just me anymore. I'm me, *plus*. You get that, right?"

His jaw tightened. "Of course."

But she still felt the need to explain. "I think I forgot, for a moment, that I can't just… act on whatever I feel. I have to consider my little family, now. And you know you don't want—"

"I understand," he said abruptly, as if to cut her off. She didn't blame him. He stood, and for a second the air around him seemed to spark with tension. But then the moment passed, and his easy charm returned. Just like that. He smiled at her, same as always. He said, "So... Not to nag, but you did mention something about jelly and a box."

It was an effort not to let her jaw drop. It was an effort not to laugh and cry at the same time. It was an effort not to get down on her fucking knees and thank him for being so *him* when she had no idea exactly who she was right now.

Instead, she offered her best approximation of a smile in return, and she put the jelly in the damn box.

By the time she opened the front door to let him out, she almost felt like herself again. She'd managed to manoeuvre her underwear back into place without him noticing—she hoped. She'd even met his eyes as they chattered about nothing—though at one point she'd imagined the phantom pressure of his lips on hers and stuttered a little.

But she was okay by the time she opened the door. The cool evening air soothed her feverish skin, and he was going now, leaving her safely alone with all this confusion and regret. She was okay.

Until he turned to her on the doorstep and said, "I'm not sorry."

She tried to wet her lips, but her tongue felt thick and dry and foreign in her mouth. "I—what?"

"You said you were sorry." Gently, he pushed her hair behind her ear. "I'm not."

Oh. Laura said something very intelligent and helpful in response, something that sounded like "Ack—ugg—wha—?"

He smiled. "Goodnight, angel."

She stood there, on the doorstep, her thoughts buzzing like a beehive, long after his headlights had faded from view.

CHAPTER NINE

DANIEL WAS GOING to kill her.

That was Laura's first thought when his eyes found hers. His green gaze was searing, venomous. His jaw was set, the tick of a leaping muscle spelling out his fury. His full lips pressed into a thin, pale line, and his alabaster skin flushed hot scarlet.

Such a handsome man, her red-headed husband. Everyone said so. They whispered behind Laura's back about how lucky she was, landing a guy like him, with his money and his looks.

Perhaps they'd have all changed their minds if they could see him like this, just once.

"You did this on purpose," he gritted out.

She wanted to shout out her indignation. She wanted to remind him that she hadn't even wanted to have *sex*, never mind get pregnant—that she hadn't wanted to touch him for months, that *he'd* insisted every time. More than insisted. But she was already humiliated enough, sitting here relying on her father-in-law to protect her. Trevor didn't need to know the terrible details of their marriage. He probably wouldn't believe her if she told him, anyway. He'd only agreed to all this—agreed to be there when she told Daniel, agreed to let her stay with him—because she had his grandchild in her belly.

"Daniel," Trevor was saying. "Control your temper—"

"What the fuck are you on her side for?" Daniel spat. "You don't know how she is. She's a manipulative, money-grabbing, false little bitch. I bet this is all a scam anyway."

"Daniel!" Trevor sounded shocked, which was rich. Didn't he know his own son by now? "Laura is your *wife*."

Laura was Daniel's verbal punching bag, actually. She could feel herself shrinking already, wilting, becoming nothing. And beneath the familiar nothingness was dread, heavy and nauseating, dragging her down toward her grave. She'd made a mistake, thinking Trevor's presence would help. She saw murder in Daniel's eyes. The hot flash of his temper couldn't be controlled. He wouldn't limit himself to lashing that barbed wire tongue. He wouldn't even be satisfied with bruising her hips and her wrists as he forced himself between her legs. Not this time.

This time, the pinches where no-one could see and the strands of her hair he pulled out would not be enough.

"You'll have an abortion," he said, his voice cold steel.

"Now, wait a minute," Trevor began gruffly.

But Daniel's monstrous temper didn't know, or perhaps didn't care, that his father held the purse strings. "Shut up!" he roared. And then, standing to his full menacing height, he turned back to Laura. And he said again, "You will have an abortion."

Laura was supposed to thank God, and count her blessings, and bow and scrape and say, *Of course I will.* He was going to let her do it properly. He was going to take her to a hospital or something, and let a doctor fix her, instead of beating her until she bled. This was a gift.

But she must've been possessed that day, because when she opened her mouth to agree, what came out was, "I will not."

She didn't know who was more shocked—him or her. He gaped, his rage replaced for a second by utter astonishment. He forgot himself entirely and deigned to argue with her. He spluttered, "Laura—you'll ruin yourself. You want to be even fatter? You want to be ugly? Don't you want to keep me happy?"

Beside her, Trevor blanched. And then his face hardened, and he stood too. He might be older than his son, but he was still a formidable man.

"Is this how you treat her?" he demanded. "Is this how you speak to your wife?"

As though she hadn't tried to tell him.

But then, Laura supposed, she shouldn't be bitter. She'd tried to tell her sister, too, and even her mother, and they'd laughed in her face. Trevor, bless him, had at least humoured her. Perversely, she was glad that Daniel was losing control. Trevor's outrage—the fact that finally, *finally*, she had a witness—gave Laura something that felt like strength. It must have been strength, in fact, because it let her stand, too, and rest a hand over her still-soft belly. It let her say, "I don't give a fuck about you. I don't give a fuck about your happiness. I'm going to your father's house, and you're going to let me. I want a divorce."

Watching Daniel's anger return was like watching one of those stop-motion captures of a garden bursting into bloom. In a matter of seconds, the seeds of his rage grew overripe fruit, flesh bursting through the skin, quicker than she could track. His gaze glittered, slithering over her like a snake over water. "If you think I'm letting you out of that door," he said softly, "you don't know me at all."

"I do know you," she murmured. "I wish I'd known you before I married you, but I know you now. I wish I'd believed in Ruth—"

"*Don't* say her name!" he exploded.

Because the sorry truth was that Laura hadn't even been her husband's first choice of captive. The victim he really wanted had escaped. And Laura, under Daniel's spell, had believed Ruth to be the problem. Oh, if only she'd known.

"You can't hurt me," she whispered.

A sick smile stretched her husband's lips. "I'm Daniel Burne. I can do whatever the fuck I want."

Oh, she remembered this. This was the part where Trevor told Daniel how things would be: "You'll see Laura under my supervision. No-one can know about the separation. We'll keep up appearances, and she'll stay with me until you can see sense…"

This was the part where Daniel ranted and raved and rammed his fist through the wall's fucking plasterboard.

This was the part where she escaped the gilded mausoleum they called home, Trevor silent and disbelieving and guilty by her side.

But for some reason, this time, it didn't happen that way. Instead, Daniel came toward her, and Trevor didn't stop him, and she couldn't move, she couldn't move—her limbs were trapped by invisible, cooling concrete. She couldn't even protect her stomach as he drew back his fist. She couldn't—she couldn't—

She woke up.

IF IT HADN'T BEEN for her screaming bladder, Laura might have stayed frozen in bed, cold sweat sliding over her face to mingle with hot tears.

But if she didn't get up, she'd piss herself. So she got up.

As she sat on the toilet staring at nothing, Laura reminded herself how it had really happened. How Daniel's fist had met nothing but a wall. How Trevor had protected her, and taken her, and let her stay in his home—even if he hadn't wanted to hear about his son's abuse, or see her bruises.

Yet. He hadn't wanted to hear yet. But he had, eventually. Ruth had helped with that.

It took a long, hot shower and several cups of tea for Laura's hands to stop shaking. Even then, she felt like a toddler's Lego tower; like something that might collapse at any moment, something that made no pretence of stability.

Something could be smashed to pieces with no effort whatsoever.

So she should've been happy when her sister called, right? Relieved, maybe. Comforted, perhaps.

She wasn't.

"Hayley," Laura said, trying her best to sound warm and calm and totally okay. She was curled up on the divan in the living room, her gaze fixed on the silent, blank TV. "How are you?"

"Oh, who cares about me? What's going on with you? Tell me everything," Hayley demanded. She was a naturally demanding sort of woman, and she liked gossip.

Laura didn't know what to say. June threatened, and so did the tourists, but tempestuous weather kept Beesley from becoming too busy. Kids hadn't broken up for the summer holidays yet, either. She still felt like she was in a sweet, seaside bubble, untouched by the outside world. Even if her bubble was a little unsettled by the distance she'd put between herself and Samir over the past two weeks. But that part had been necessary.

Hadn't it?

"I'm good," Laura said, barely feeling like a liar at all. She *was* good. Way better than she'd been with Daniel. Not as great as she'd felt around Samir. "Not much has happened since you last called. Midwife keeps banging on about my BMI."

"Maybe you should listen," Hayley said. "It's not good for the baby, you being so inactive."

Laura sighed. "You know I swim every day."

"Mmm," Hayley murmured. Laura's sister was fond of the sort of exercise regime that gave one rock-hard abs and toned thighs. She had this strange idea that since Laura's belly was soft and her thighs pillow-like, she did nothing but lie around drinking whipped cream through a straw.

Laura didn't have the energy to argue about it, so she was glad when Hayley changed the subject. "What have you been *up to*, though? You barely said anything last time I called."

"I haven't got much to say, lovely. I'm relaxing."

"Think of something," Hayley said flatly. "Mum's getting on my nerves, asking for information. Although, if *you'd* speak to her—"

"I *do* speak to her," Laura interrupted calmly. She'd gotten better at that, in her weeks staying with Trevor. Better at standing up for herself, being firm. The way she used to be.

She could almost hear her sister's eye roll through the phone. "You know what I mean. You tell her the bare minimum."

"Just because she wants to be Mother of the Year all of a sudden," Laura said crisply, "doesn't mean I have to let her." And then, before the argument lurking beneath that conversation's surface could ferment, she changed the subject. "I've made a friend."

"You have?"

"Yeah. Her name's Kelly. She's a waitress at this cafe I go to." *This cafe I go to,* because for some reason, Laura still hadn't told her sister about Samir.

Why? She had no idea. She had no reason to hold Samir close like a hot water bottle on a cold night. Maybe it was because he starred in her good dreams as predictably as Daniel starred in her nightmares. Or because he kept smiling and bringing her omelettes and asking about the baby, even though she'd stopped showing up to their midnight meetings.

Or because she'd given up trying to forget the way he touched her, the way he made her feel like a goddess and a woman all at once.

"A waitress?" Hayley squawked, her sharp incredulity

smashing through Laura's thoughts. "Since when do you befriend waitresses?"

Laura opened her mouth, then shut it again. "I... well, I don't know. She's nice. Really funny, and sweet. And she's also a waitress. Does it matter?"

"Does it *matter*? Don't you remember at your rehearsal dinner, that waiter tried to give me his number and you—"

"Don't."

But Hayley didn't hear the faintly murmured word, or maybe didn't care. "You called the manager and complained about the *staff* harassing your sister? You called him *uppity*!"

Laura remembered.

You would think, with the number of awful things she'd done in her life, that they'd all blur together. But she remembered every desperate, acidic moment. Her stomach became lead and her skin tightened, hot and prickly as if covered by insects. Her morning sickness had stopped weeks ago, but she felt familiar nausea congealing in her gut and saliva pooling on her tongue. She remembered the look on the boy's face—because he had been just a boy. A teenager, no older than Kelly's Daisy, and he'd slipped Hayley his number without a word or even a look after they'd spent the whole meal flirting.

Laura wanted to cry, but she had nothing to cry about. Monsters shouldn't take all the tears.

Hayley didn't seem to be struggling at all. In fact, she was laughing. As if this was a happy memory. As if this was so fucking funny. She'd laughed at the time, too, along with Laura. And all the while, Laura had felt Daniel's gaze on her, heavy and approving—for now. And she'd hoped that maybe he'd be kind to her that evening, maybe he'd admire her instead of seeing only her flaws.

"I shouldn't have done that," Laura mumbled, but she could barely hear herself over Hayley's chuckles. So she repeated it, louder, sure this time. "I shouldn't have done that. It wasn't funny."

The laughter faded. "So why did you?" Hayley demanded, immediately belligerent.

"Because... because..." Laura released a breath, and then the words came in a reckless torrent. "Because I was afraid that the whole thing would remind Daniel how I used to waitress. You remember? And he doesn't like to think about that, or for people to know." The Albrights were supposed to be the Burnes' equals, Ravenswood royalty just like Daniel. She knew now that her name was the only reason he'd taken her in the first place.

And he'd wanted desperately to hide her family's little blips. The things nobody talked about. The fact that her parents had poured the Albright funds down a drain called drink when Laura was just a kid, and she'd been fighting secretly to survive ever since.

She'd succeeded, too. She'd dragged herself back up to the position her family deserved. And when the staff got too comfortable, Laura skewered them. Better that than allow anyone to remember she'd once *been* them.

At least, that was how she used to think.

"Look," she sighed, because Hayley's silence was a little too stretched-out and sullen for her liking. "All I'm saying is, we could both stand to climb off our pedestals. It wasn't that long ago I was waitressing to put us through uni. We don't have to act like we've always been this way."

"Don't start getting all *We the people*," Hayley snapped. "You never minded spending Daniel's money."

Laura swallowed down her bile. If her sister was... *unpleasant* sometimes, well, that might be Laura's fault. She was the one who'd raised Hayley. She was the one who'd spent years being a stuck-up, smug, superior bitch.

And now she was trying to be Little Miss Perfect, just because she'd seen the error of her ways. Wasn't that stuck-up, smug and superior all over again?

"You're right," she sighed. "I'm sorry."

There was a pause before Hayley sniffed, "Don't worry about it. Listen, I've got to go, okay?"

"Okay." Laura tried not to feel relieved. It was disloyal.

"Bye, sis. Love you."

"Love you." She put the phone down and stared at the blank TV, and wondered what love really meant.

CHAPTER TEN

"Samir."

There was nothing so satisfying as the sharp slice and firm *thwack* of a knife gliding through onion to hit a chopping board. Samir made the sound again and again, pounding out a beat that matched his heavy pulse and grinding teeth, slashing the onion to pieces and ignoring his stinging eyes.

"Samir."

Some people might say that the diced slithers of onion beneath his hands were too fine to be further attacked, but those people just weren't committed enough. Or determined enough.

Or frustrated enough.

"*Samir.*"

Focus destroyed. Rhythm blown. The blade faltered, then glided across the side of Samir's thumb, spilling thin, tomato-red blood all over his fucking onions.

"Shit," he hissed, sticking his thumb in his mouth. Gross. Onion and blood was, it turned out, a horrible combination.

Samir turned to glare at the man who'd thrown off his concentration. Max arched a brow in the face of his boss's mightiest glower, patently unaffected.

"Cut yourself?" he asked, as if he didn't know.

"Nah," Samir said. "I'm just sucking my thumb cuz I'm still seven years old."

Max's second eyebrow rose to join the first. "You sucked your thumb 'til you were seven years old?"

"Jesus, man, what do you want?"

"I want to know what's going on with you." Max folded his arms and leaned back against the gleaming, steel counter, his eyes as careful as his posture was relaxed. "You good?"

Those two words were heavy as stone and soft as marshmallows all at once. *You good?* It was the question they'd agreed, years back, to ask each other regularly. A question they'd agreed to answer honestly, too. Always.

And yet, something thick and uncomfortable lodged in Samir's throat when he tried to tell the truth. Even as the tension drained from his muscles and the pointless, pent-up irritation dissolved from his bloodstream, he couldn't force out what was on his mind.

What came out instead surprised even him. "You really love Daisy."

Max's expression didn't change, despite the random subject. "Of course I do. She's my daughter."

"That's what I mean. She..." Samir cleared his throat, moving to the sink to wash his hands. The cut was starting to sting.

And if the action allowed him to avoid his best friend's careful eyes, well, that was just a coincidence.

"She was—what, seven, when you met Kelly?" Samir asked, trying to keep his tone light. He succeeded, too. His voice was raw and ragged as one of Max's serrated blades, but it was light as fuckin' air.

"She was six," Max said. "Same age as Poppy is now." Poppy being the third of his and Kelly's children. They were really committed to the floral thing.

Samir nodded. "Right. So... when you met Kelly, how did you feel about—I mean, she had a kid, and you didn't. Did that ever worry you?"

"No," Max said. "It might have. If Kelly was just another woman, it might have. If I'd met her, liked her, wanted to get to know her and find out where things led... maybe I'd have hesitated. I don't know."

"But you didn't?" Samir pulled a first aid box out of the cupboard, rifling through it for a plaster. "Hesitate, I mean."

"No."

"Why not?"

"You gonna look at me?" Max's voice was gentle. This, Samir knew, was how he spoke to his girls. Samir was getting the baby voice. That realisation alone was enough to make him straighten up and turn around.

Max was still leaning against the counter, looking as if he had all the time in the world to talk to Samir about the events of years ago.

To be fair, the cafe was pretty quiet now the afternoon rush had passed. But still.

"Well?" Samir asked, the harshness of his own voice

driving away his gnat-like worries. "Why didn't you hesitate?"

Max smiled slightly. "Because with Kelly, I didn't want to see where it went. I knew where it was going. I loved her. I didn't want anything but her. And since I loved her so much, how could I not love Daisy?"

Samir swallowed down the lump in his throat. "So you just... became a father. Just like that."

Max shrugged. "I could've knocked some girl up and become a father *just like that.* I chose to become a father. Wasn't an instant process, but it was an instant commitment. I made the choice. That was it."

"You weren't... anxious?"

"Probably no more anxious than a single woman waiting to give birth to her first child alone." That statement was followed by a less-than-subtle look. "The only difference is that no-one ever made me feel guilty for my worries. I was allowed nerves, I was permitted hesitation. It was only natural." He shrugged. "People don't seem to make those same allowances for the ones carrying the babies."

Samir nodded slowly. He knew himself; knew that it would take a while for those words to sink into his brain, and even longer for him to sort through them and decide what they meant. Or rather, what they meant for him. So he filed the conversation away. Let it sit, brewing like a good, strong cup of tea.

"I didn't see Laura today," Max said. "That why you're attacking my onions?"

"Don't worry about me and Laura," Samir muttered, moving to clear up the mess he'd left on the chopping board.

"You say that," Max murmured wryly, "but over the last couple of weeks... You two are avoiding each other, which can't be easy since you've been inseparable since April—"

"I wouldn't say *inseparable*."

"I would. You're like magnets. Even when you're not connected, anyone can see that something's pulling you together."

Those softly spoken words had Samir frowning so hard, he started to give himself a headache. "Don't you have orders to cook or something?"

"Shut up, boy. When she's here, you barely speak, and when she isn't, you wander into my kitchen and start slicing shit up like you're plotting a murder."

"Don't say that." He wrapped a blue plaster around his thumb, shut the first aid kit, and turned to meet Max's eye. "You make it sound like I'm angry at her."

"Aren't you?"

"No. Of course not. She hasn't done anything wrong."

Max's brows arched. "Have you?"

Ah. There, Samir faltered. "I don't know. I'm not sure. Maybe."

"Why don't you ask her? Then you'll be sure."

Ask her? He couldn't just ask her. Two weeks ago, he'd ruined everything. He'd practically mauled her on her kitchen table. She'd stopped showing up to their midnight meetings, and every time she saw him all she could do was blush and stutter. But it suddenly occurred to Samir that Laura *did* still see him. She still came into the cafe almost every day, just like she had before. She didn't have to do that. Surely, she wouldn't do that if he made her uncomfortable. Would she?

He'd know the answer to that question if he asked her.

It was as if Samir had spent the last two weeks under a permanent storm cloud, only for his best friend to blow it away like so much dust.

"There we go," Max grinned. "That's what I like to see!"

And Samir realised he was smiling.

IN EARLY JUNE, the beach should be half-full of tourists. Today, though, a storm threatened. The weather was cool, and the sea's spray even cooler. So it was quiet as he strode across the sand toward the beach house.

Max was locking up, so Samir had left early to wander the shore like a particularly obvious stalker. He'd never seen Laura on the beach in daylight, as opposed to moonlight, but it occurred to him that she might be out here despite the cold. She always had loved the ocean, and she lived so close. He could see the beach house in the distance now, its blue-painted wood panels bright against the grey skies.

Grey skies which, rather embarrassingly, made him think about Laura's eyes. Jesus. Next thing, he'd be writing bloody sonnets.

He turned his gaze resolutely toward the ocean—and that was when he saw it. A flash of movement in the distance, a pale figure floating out at sea. Worry gripped him. The wind was picking up, and the water out here was deeper than it seemed. He wasn't close enough to tell if the figure was just swimming, or if they needed help, or if it was a person at all. But Samir was speeding up before he'd even made the conscious decision, jogging and then running over the sand, the bobbing figure drawing closer and closer. It *was* a person, he realised. A person floating aimlessly along in a way that might be therapeutic, but could also be dangerous.

He picked up the pace, and slowly, details came into focus. One specific detail caught him, though; strands of long hair picked up by the wind, lashing at the sky like dark ribbons.

It was ridiculous, and yet... "Laura?" he shouted. But he didn't expect her, or whoever it was, to hear him over the growing *whoosh* of the waves. He wasn't close enough. So he saved his breath and ran harder, the sand shifting beneath his feet, the quickening wind sending a rush of wild sensation through him in the way that only seaside wind could. His muscles pumped tirelessly, but he felt as if he were barely moving. Jesus, he needed to start jogging on the beach more.

It seemed like he drew close enough to see her all at once. It *was* Laura, eyes closed, fully-clothed, from the looks of things, and bobbing around like a fucking buoy. Shit. Shit shit shit. A cruel fist twisted around his heart as he kicked off his shoes and ran into the water.

The sea became a living thing insistent on shoving him from its embrace. He thrust against the force, making an arrow of his body, slicing through the waves as best he could. Saltwater flew into his eyes, occasionally finding its way up his nose. His technique was sloppy. No; his technique was frantic. He'd swum in this ocean countless times, but all of a sudden it was like his legs had forgotten how to fucking kick.

And yet, somehow, he managed. He powered through

the waves and reached her eventually, if not fast enough for his liking. When she was still a few metres away, he spat out a mouthful of sea and shouted, "Laura!"

And, miracle of miracles, she opened her eyes. Her surprise was as clear as the tendrils of water-black hair plastered against her skin. "Samir?"

Another second, and he had her. His hand closed around her wrist, even though he could tell, from this close, that she was actually fine. She was fine. But his heartbeat, wild as the ocean around them, didn't seem ready to accept that message.

He dragged her toward him through the water, too hard and too close. He shouldn't be pulling her into his chest or pressing his forehead against hers, or running his hands over her face as if to check she was still there. But here he was, doing all of that ridiculous shit and more.

"Jesus Christ," he panted. "I thought you passed out or something! I thought you were drowning."

She paled. "I'm sorry. I just—"

"You're too far out! You shouldn't be so far out when no-one's on the beach!"

"I'm a really good swimmer," she said, her tone soothing. "Like, really, really good. I can swim anywhere."

"I know that!" He was overreacting. He knew he was overreacting. She was pregnant, for God's sake; she wouldn't take on more than she could handle. She'd be careful.

But he wanted her to be *more* careful. With everything. Always. You know, just in case.

"I'm sorry," he said finally. "I... I just, I saw you and I thought you—"

"It's okay," she said. "It's okay. I'm fine. See?" She smiled, and he felt her cheeks plump up beneath his hands—which reminded him that, oh, shit, he was still holding her face. He let go, but she put an arm around his shoulder and they floated there for a moment, alone in the ocean's vast jaws. His heart, gradually, slowed.

"Let's go back to the beach," she said, and even though he'd come crashing to her rescuing, it felt like she was the one looking after him. He nodded, and her answering smile was gentle, soothing.

For once, he felt like being soothed.

She hadn't lied about being a good swimmer. Hell, Samir was a good swimmer, but she cut through the waves ahead of him with effortless speed and strength, as if she belonged to the sea. When the shore grew close enough for her to stand, watching her emerge, dripping-wet, in her clinging, black dress was like watching a mermaid transform. Almost unnatural, but beautiful, too.

She sat on the sand and watched him come to join her with a smile, wringing out her hair. It was long enough that the action drew his eye toward her hips, and then, through the soaking-wet fabric of her clothes, to the prominent curve of her stomach.

The reminder of her pregnancy should've cooled the white-hot flame she ignited in him. It didn't.

It did, however, piss him off.

He sat beside her and started scolding all over again, as if he'd never stopped. "You shouldn't have gone out there alone. I don't care how good a swimmer you are. You could —you could faint! Pregnant people faint all the time. And then you'd drown."

He saw her lips twitch slightly, but she murmured, "You're right."

"Or you could get a cramp and... sink... or something."

"I could." She nodded solemnly.

He scowled. "For fuck's sake. If you want to go floating off into the ocean, call me first, okay? Call me, and I'll come and watch you."

Her brows rose slightly. With her hair sleek and mirror-shiny, her cheeks whipped pink by the wind, and her lashes dripping salt-water crystals, she looked like a mermaid all over again.

Like a siren.

"You'd come just to watch me swim?" she asked.

"I'd come to keep you safe."

Her smile faded. "I don't need a keeper."

He couldn't hold back his snort at the idea. "Of course you don't. But sometimes you might..." He trailed off, shrugging. "Sometimes you might want a partner."

Her eyes widened slightly, as if she'd seen something she'd never seen before. Samir watched her lips part, then press together, then part again. Her fingers sank into the sand between them. She looked out to the sea, down at her lap—or rather, at her bump—and then back to him.

She started to speak.

And then, of course, the heavens opened.

CHAPTER ELEVEN

RUNNING over sand in a thunderstorm would be easier if her stomach didn't resemble an especially heavy beach ball. Laura was kind of struggling—until Samir put an arm around her, and caught her hand with his free one, and practically pushed her along. And just like that, they ran. She was barefoot and already drenched, and the wind dragged her hair across her face in a wet slap every chance it got. But despite all that, she laughed.

It must have taken them a while to reach the house's back porch, but it felt like no time at all. She almost slipped as her feet met the cold tiles, but he caught her. His arm came around her from behind like a steel bar, somehow fitting into the non-existent space between her swollen belly and her equally swollen breasts. Then his *other* arm slid around her hips, and his hot breath ghosted over her cold neck, and she felt...

"Alright?" he asked softly.

"Yes," she said, sounding far too precise, way too sharp, to be believable. She should've been flustered or winded or panicked, because that would've made sense. But she sounded perfect—and he would know exactly what that meant, by now. Somehow, over these past months, he'd learned her all over again.

So Laura didn't look back as he released her slowly, his hands hovering inches from her hips. Instead, she kept her eyes on the door, fumbling with the unlocked latch like a ninny before pushing it open and stepping inside.

"I have some old clothes that should fit you," she said, flicking on the hall light. "We're about the same—" She turned in time to see Samir dragging his T-shirt up over his head. Her words died in her throat.

Oh. Oh, Lord. The cotton was so sodden, he had to peel it off in slow-motion—or at least, it *felt* like slow-motion. There was a moment when his arms were raised over his head, and the dark fabric covered his face, and she could just... stare without shame. So she did, of course. Ohhh, yes, she did.

Even though she knew she shouldn't.

His body wasn't the sort of thing you saw on TV. It wasn't the sort of thing heartthrobs posted on Instagram, either, and it certainly didn't resemble her husband's carefully maintained six pack. Samir looked like a guy who just happened to be built on a large scale. He was *solid*—that was the word that dominated her mind. Thick-waisted, barrel-chested, biceps bulging. His torso was covered in dark hair that trailed like an arrow down his stomach, disappearing beneath the waistband of his jeans.

Oh, the jeans were wet too. And his thighs were just as solid as the rest of him. And between those thighs—

Good Lord. Her mouth went dry. All the moisture that belonged to her lips appeared to have relocated. South.

"Laura?"

Fuck. He sounded surprised enough that she had no doubt: he'd caught her staring. *Staring* was probably too tame a word, actually. She could feel the heavy rise and fall of her own chest as her breathing quickened, and she knew she was blushing. She had to be. Her skin felt hot and cold all at once. Had she always had a heartbeat between her legs?

She should probably tear her eyes away from the outline of his dick now. Yeah. That was a great idea.

She looked up, but not at him. God, she couldn't look at him. Laura focused her gaze on the door behind his head and babbled, "I have clothes you can wear bathroom's upstairs on the right spare towels in—"

"Laura." He stepped toward her, and then hesitated because—oh, God, had she just squeaked? Like a mouse? A perverted, guilty mouse?

"I'm pregnant!" she blurted.

"So I hear." He had the audacity to sound *amused*. She had a feeling that, if she looked at his face, he'd be smiling. He was probably laughing at her. Of course he was laughing at her.

"I just meant—pregnant people do… odd things…"

"It's kind of funny how you use pregnancy as an excuse for everything you do."

"What?"

"Also, when you say *odd things*, do you mean staring at my crotch? Because—"

She had died. She had died of embarrassment and this conversation was hell.

"Because I wasn't entirely sure that you *were* staring at my crotch, but now I am. Next time, I'd advise silence or denial."

Her gaze flew to his without permission from her brain. He was, as she'd expected, smiling. But it wasn't the smile she was used to.

No—it *was*. It was exactly the smile she was used to from Samir. Genuine, and real, and wonderful. But she'd been expecting someone else's, harsh and mocking and cruel.

"God, you're such a fucking idiot, Laura. I really don't know why I'm with you."

She swallowed hard, sucking in a breath and pushing back the memory. "I'm... I'm sorry. I'm really sorry. I don't know *what* came over me."

"You know you sound different when you apologise?"

She bit her lip. "Different how?"

"I don't know. But I don't like it." Before she could even *begin* to understand that, he spoke again. "You're shivering. I don't like that either. Let's go upstairs."

The words traced mockingly over her skin, like a touch she couldn't quite feel. If she hadn't had goosebumps already, they'd have appeared everywhere. Which was ridiculous, because by *Let's go upstairs*, he meant *Let's get dry*. Not, *I'm going to ravish you now*. This wasn't a bloody romance novel. They had both agreed that there would be absolutely no more ravishing.

But he didn't really agree at all, did he?

"Come on. You need a hot shower at least." He twisted his T-shirt into a loose, thick sort of rope, then slung it around his shoulders. His *bare* shoulders. His bare, broad shoulders.

Concentrate!

"You go," she said stiffly, sweeping scraps of dignity about her like a patchwork cloak. She couldn't be around him right now, that much was clear. "I need to dry the floor so the wood doesn't lift."

"Fuck that. If you get pneumonia, the baby gets pneumonia."

Laura opened her mouth to argue, but then remembered that he was actually right. She did *not* want her baby to get pneumonia. Even if she wasn't entirely sure that pneumonia worked that way. But then, what did she know about pneumonia? Nothing. Literally nothing. Could she even *spell* pneumonia? Had she ever tried? No. And now her baby was going to get pneumonia because she'd wasted time staring at Samir Bianchi's dick. Daniel had been right about one thing; she'd make a terrible mother.

"Hey," Samir said, and she jerked back to reality as he reached for her. He brushed his knuckles over her cheek, slow and soft. It should be comforting. It shouldn't feel like he was sending surges of electricity through her nerve-endings, and it shouldn't cause her nipples to tingle in a way that had nothing to do with pregnancy. But it really, really did. "You okay?" he asked gently.

"I'm fine," she lied. It sounded like a lie, too. She'd never been so obvious before. But when he touched her like this, and when he looked at her with so much tenderness... well, how could she not sound a little breathless?

"You sure?" He seemed kind of breathless too. Which was... interesting. His tongue slid out to wet his lower lip, and she followed the glide of that pink tip over his soft, full mouth the way she might watch for an oasis in a drought.

She'd read about this online. Pregnancy hormones. Hyper-sexuality, or whatever. She was just *generally* horny. It had nothing to do with him specifically. That was what she told herself, even as her eyes devoured every inch of his exposed skin. Then the hand stroking her cheek moved, and suddenly he was cupping the back of her neck with one big, warm palm. He groaned, and his eyes slid shut as he said, "Oh, Laura. Don't look at me like that."

She stiffened and stepped back, ignoring the fact that it was almost painful to break that perfect contact. He felt natural. He felt comforting. He felt divine. But she felt... fuck.

"Don't look at me like that". Jesus, how embarrassing. She opened her mouth to let him know that she wasn't *looking* at him at all, thank you very much, because why *would* she, as if *he* was something special—

Only she couldn't. And not just because that was old Laura, Daniel's Laura, and she was all new and entirely herself. Not even because anything she said right now, other than *Holy shit, I want you on my kitchen table again*, would be a lie. No. She couldn't do it because, even in that instinctive, mortified moment when all she wanted to do was lash out, she couldn't bring herself to slice him open and watch him bleed.

Instead, she found herself whispering, "I'm sorry." Her voice was a ghost of itself, cracked and shrunken.

He came toward her again, closing the gap she'd just created, and pulled her back into his arms—much more firmly, this time. She felt his fingers slide into her hair, angling her head until she was forced to look up at him.

What she saw was... surprising. Dark eyes burning and melting all at once, brow pleated into a frown, cheeks flushed.

"Don't," he murmured. "You don't need to apologise with me."

Laura had a feeling that if she spoke right now, something ridiculous would come out. So she kept her mouth shut.

Which turned out to be a good decision, because he added, "You know, it's hard enough not to want you when you're sitting in the cafe, minding your fucking business, barely remembering that I exist. But when you look at me like that, Laura..."

"Like what?" she whispered.

"Like you're hungry." He closed his eyes, seeming almost pained for a moment. Then he muttered, "Fuck it," and dragged her even closer, until she could count each of his long, dark lashes and see her own reflection in his eyes.

She should've felt conscious of her belly jutting between them, but all she could feel was her own pounding heart, and the unapologetic heat of his hands. His chest felt like a melting slab of ice, rain-wetness soaking through the fabric of her equally drenched dress. Laura's enormous bra was thick as cardboard, and yet her nipples tightened as if she'd brushed them directly over the rough whorls of his chest hair. Which she kind of desperately wished she could do. Could she take her bra off without him noticing?

…Probably not. Definitely not.

"I want to kiss you," he said, his voice low and hoarse. His eyes closed with a sweep of those impossible lashes, and then he was too close for her to really see—she only felt him, his nose brushing hers, his words dancing over her lips, an inch away. "I'm *going* to kiss you. Tell me not to."

She didn't.

His mouth took hers with the same easy confidence she always felt in his touch. But if she'd expected him to lick and bite and suck and own her, she was mistaken. Instead, he pressed his lips against hers as if he wanted to sink into her bones, to imprint himself on her in every possible way. No heat, no tongue, just the soft, cool comfort of his rain-wet mouth, lush and full and heart-stoppingly *him*.

He pulled back enough to repeat, "Tell me." Then there was another kiss, and her blood became too warm for her icy skin. She shivered, but it wasn't the temperature. He cradled her skull as if she were a precious, fragile thing he'd waited centuries to hold. He kissed her as if he loved her.

Fuck. He kissed her as if he loved her.

She remembered, all at once, how he'd kissed her years ago, and she wanted to cry because she'd missed him. She hadn't even realised until this very second how much she'd missed him.

Oh, she was in trouble. She was in so much trouble, and she wouldn't change a thing.

"I'm letting you go now," he murmured.

Don't you dare.

"I am," he repeated, though she hadn't spoken aloud. "I'm

letting you go." What he actually did was pull her into a hug, all warm and firm, but loose enough that she could push him away. Which would be the sensible option, of course. But Laura wasn't sensible—she was, in fact, utterly without sense, since he'd kissed it all away—so she let her head fall against his shoulder instead. Why? She had no idea. Maybe because the tears pricking her eyelids were fading, and breathing him in—the scent of cool salt, and skin, and Samir— helped speed up the process.

He rubbed one broad palm over her back in soothing circles and said, "Go upstairs, angel. Please?"

"I can't."

He took a deep breath before speaking again. "Why not?"

"Well, you're... holding on to me."

Just like that, the tension in his hard body dissolved. He released her, his face splitting into that familiar grin. "Oh, yeah. Sorry."

"It's okay."

"No, it's not." He was still smiling, but something about him seemed serious again. "Go on. Go and get warmed up."

"Okay," she said slowly. "Um... towels are in the airing cupboard on the landing. Just help yourself. I'll lay out some clothes in my room for you."

He grunted in response, which was slightly alarming, because Samir wasn't a grunting kind of guy.

She watched as he turned and wandered away from her, running a hand through his hair. His back, unfortunately, wasn't any less appealing than his chest. She'd never thought of backs as particularly interesting, but the play of muscle beneath his skin, the expanse of pure, uninterrupted nakedness, was making her decidedly warm.

And now she was lusting over his poor, innocent back while he stood around muttering to himself. She'd apparently broken Samir and she barely even felt bad about it. Oh dear.

It was definitely time to go upstairs.

CHAPTER TWELVE

LAURA WOULDN'T HAVE PICKED up the phone, only she thought it was Ruth.

Which was, in hindsight, ridiculous. Ruth never called. Ruth *hated* phone conversations. She was a text-only kind of girl.

But Ruth also had this uncanny knack for knowing exactly when Laura was having an emotional wobble, and sending a perfect... what did she call them? Memes? A perfect meme, or whatever, to make Laura smile.

So when Laura got out of the shower, and put on her pyjamas in the en-suite, and tried not to think about Samir showering somewhere in her house, or Samir kissing her, or what all of these feelings *meant*, the trill of her phone *should've* been Ruth. It should've been Ruth coming to rescue her from emotional free-fall.

It wasn't.

"Why aren't you answering my texts?"

Laura sighed. "Hi, Hayley."

"I'm serious. What's going on with you?"

"Nothing's going on with me." Laura put her phone on speaker, set it on the counter, and picked up a hairbrush. She was certain she'd need to keep her hands occupied during this conversation.

"So why are you ignoring me?"

"Hayley. We spoke this morning. Like, eight hours ago. What more could I possibly have to tell you?"

Her sister gave a derisive snort. "I know you texted Trevor today. You're always texting him. It's weird."

"He's my father-in-law."

"Not for long."

"He's my baby's grandpa. And what do you mean *not for long*?" Her heart leapt. "Has Daniel changed his mind? Is he signing the Acknowledgement?"

She would've been divorced months ago, if her husband would accept the fucking petition. But even though he despised her, even though he didn't want her baby, even though he'd hissed the words at her a thousand times, he refused to sign. Because of him, they had to do things the hard way.

He *claimed* he didn't want her taking half of his money. Which was ridiculous, since the money was his father's anyway.

Hayley's voice was heavy as a baby's thrust-out bottom lip and twice as petulant. "How am I supposed to know?"

Laura sighed. "I don't know. Sorry. It was just the way you said it—"

"Oh, whatever. Look, babe, I think you should come home."

The hairbrush caught on a particularly tight tangle in

Laura's hair. She winced as it dragged at her scalp. Bump chose that moment to wake up and dance about, which made her feel slightly nauseated, desperate to wee, and kind of comforted, too. "Home?"

"Yeah. Back to Ravenswood."

Funny, but the word *home* didn't command images of the town she'd spent most of her life in. For some reason, when Laura thought of home, she thought of here. The beach house. The kitchen. The table. With Samir sitting—

Okay, that was enough of that.

"I told you," Laura murmured, easing the brush through her tangled hair. "I'm staying here. It's relaxing. Anyway, you and Mum will be here in September, right?"

"Well, that's the thing," Hayley sighed. "I spoke to Mum, and she doesn't think it's a good idea. She doesn't want to come."

Laura blinked. In the mirror, her reflection's flat gaze lit up. Her lips spread into a genuine smile. The Laura in the mirror looked happy. Relieved, actually. Laura knew how she felt.

"That's fine," she said, trying to sound bravely disappointed as opposed to bloody ecstatic. "I don't mind. It'll be just the two of us." She put down her hairbrush and picked up the phone, taking it off speaker. Presumably, her sister didn't want to hear the sound of an incredibly long pregnancy-wee. "Actually, I was thinking maybe—and I don't know if she'd even be okay with this, but maybe—Ruth could come too?"

Silence. Silence that stretched out for so long, Laura started to wonder if the line had gone dead. So long that she'd actually finished on the toilet by the time Hayley spoke in a voice charred and crackling. "Seriously?"

"Yeah. What do you think?"

"What do I think?" Hayley hissed.

Ah. So she wasn't on board, then.

"You want that *bitch* to be there when *Daniel's* baby is born?"

Laura's brows shot up. A sick sort of dread began to coalesce low in her gut, like storm clouds forming over the sea. She recognised that dread, the one that sent her skin crawling in fearful anticipation, but she didn't understand why it was coming now. This was her sister, after all. Just her sister. Hayley might be a brat sometimes, but she wouldn't hurt Laura. She *couldn't* hurt Laura.

"First of all," she replied, trying to keep her voice calm, "this is not Daniel's baby. He's made it very clear that he wants zero involvement. This is *my* baby."

Hayley snorted.

Laura talked right over that snort for the sake of her temper. The dismissal made her blood boil. "Secondly," she said, her voice firmer now, "don't call Ruth a bitch. Don't call any woman a bitch."

"Oh, you're a feminist now? That's cute."

Laura's jaw dropped. "What the fuck?"

"You can't lecture me!" Hayley snapped. The walls of the bathroom, with their old-fashioned, hand-painted tiles; the expensive skincare products Daniel had paid for lined up on the counter—they all seemed to grow larger. And all the while, Laura grew smaller. Her surroundings closed in as she shrank in response to the hate dripping from her sister's voice. "You *despised* Ruth. And you should! She slept with your husband—"

"That is *not* what happened," Laura managed, but her voice came out thin and reedy.

"Oh, now you believe her bullshit? She's a fat, desperate, attention-seeking slut—"

"Hayley! Ruth was your *friend.*"

"When I was, like, five. I grew up. You should too. Daniel is an amazing man, and you know what? I am officially sick of how you're treating him."

"What?" The word was a disbelieving whisper, a shattered breath that Hayley probably didn't even hear. She was too busy bulldozing over Laura's heart.

"He's given you everything, and you throw a tantrum over a fucking baby? And take *Ruth's* side just to spite him? Where is your loyalty, Laura?"

"Are you serious? Hayley, I told you how he—"

"I know what you told me," Hayley snapped. "I don't believe you."

The words were like a fist to the face. They were the punch Laura had dreamt of that very morning, the one she'd barely escaped by waking up.

She was wide awake now. There was no way to evade this particular pain.

Still, she leant against the bathroom wall, as though the touch of cool, hard tiles to her feverish cheek might ease the sting of that betrayal.

"I don't believe you."

Daniel had told her. He'd told her countless times, with open glee, that no-one would believe her. But—but Trevor believed her. Daniel's own father. Surely Hayley—Hayley, who Laura had practically raised, who she'd given up her teenage years for, who she'd grown up too fast for, who she'd cooked for and scrimped and saved for and smiled for when she felt like crying...

Surely Hayley believed her? Surely Hayley *had* to believe her? That's what sisters *did*.

And yet, a little voice whispered in Laura's ear, *Why didn't you tell her first, then? Why didn't you tell her years ago, when it all began? Why didn't she ever seem to hear you, when you tried to say the words?*

The hot, sick, sticky feeling in Laura's gut swelled. She didn't want to face the answer, but it forced its way into her head, and it felt like Daniel used to. Like contamination.

She was never going to protect you.

"I don't believe you," Hayley repeated, sounding calmer now, more sure of herself. Almost proud, as if she'd overcome something by saying those words out loud. "You're a liar. You just want Daniel's money. He's a good man, and he loved you. You've broken his heart, doing all this. Lying like this. Turning his own father against him, running off with his baby—"

"Hayley." The tears running down Laura's cheeks threatened to choke her, reducing her voice to a wiry whisper, but she had to get the words out. "Hayley, don't trust him. Don't fall for him. He'll hurt you."

"I... I don't know what you're talking about," Hayley stammered, her sharp-edged confidence faltering for the first time.

Laura didn't have the patience for her sister's tired denials. All she had now was pain and disbelief and fear.

"Please don't trust him. You don't know what he's like. He doesn't love you—"

"Shut up," Hayley said, voice a jagged blade.

"He doesn't. He just needs someone to hurt—"

"SHUT UP!" The roar was so loud, so violent, Laura almost dropped the phone. "You're a liar," Hayley spat. "You're a manipulative, jealous bitch. You don't care about me. You don't care about anyone but yourself. You don't want him to be happy."

"Hayley, I am your *sister*."

"You're an ungrateful gold digger," her little sister hissed down the phone, "and I'm done talking to you."

A spark of white-hot fury cut through Laura's disbelief. "Well, you know what?" she managed. "I am done with you too. *Done*, Hayley."

The line went dead. And her beautiful, buoyant anger died with it, leaving behind nothing but pain.

All of a sudden, even the icy kiss of the bathroom tiles was too much. Everything was sweaty and heavy and burning-hot—too direct and too painful and...

Fuck, she was suffocating. She couldn't breathe.

Laura fumbled with the lock on the door, clumsy hands forcing it open. She practically fell out of the room, and as she stumbled, a familiar pair of arms caught her.

Her head jerked up. Samir was looking down at her with this heartbreaking concern in his deep, dark eyes, white teeth worrying his lower lip, her NTU T-shirt straining over his chest. Laura realized that she felt like she was suffocating because she was sobbing so hard, crying so much, heaving in gasping, desperate breaths as tears and snot and pure hysteria teamed up to steal her oxygen.

Also, she'd been wrong to think her clothes would fit Samir. He made her T-shirt look like body-con.

She laughed mid-sob and almost choked to death on her own snot bubble.

"Shit," he said, not in a *Good God, how disgusting* sort of way, but more of an *Oh no, this baby bird has been run over, how sad and disgusting* sort of way. It was a crucial difference.

Then he picked her up. Like, *picked her up.* She didn't have the energy to complain, or worry, or feel self-conscious, or even enjoy it.

She felt like she'd never enjoy anything again.

"I don't believe you."

Laura closed her eyes as if doing so could block out the memory of those poisonous words. She felt Samir put her down on the bed, and then she rolled over, sinking into a pile of soft pillows. Maybe, if she kept her eyes shut and stayed very still forever, she could turn to stone.

Only she'd definitely need the toilet before that happened. Like, a thousand times.

And, wait—she couldn't turn to stone, because then Bump would never be born. She couldn't even turn to stone *after* Bump was born, because who would look after them?

No-one. Bump only had Laura.

The thought was sobering enough to calm her gulping sobs.

"Hey," Samir said. He'd left a moment ago, she thought, but now here he was, coming back. *Being* back. Or something.

Her brain was fuzzy.

He pulled her onto her back, and she flopped over like a doll. Kept her eyes closed, too. Overwhelming despair was starting to fade, which allowed room for other emotions, like embarrassment, to creep in.

But as long as she closed her eyes, and couldn't see him, she could pretend that he couldn't see her. Right? Wasn't that how things worked?

She heard Ruth's dry voice in her head, saying simply, "*Nope*".

Then she felt tissue pressed against her nose, which was a surprise.

"Blow," Samir said.

Laura's eyes flew open.

He was sitting beside her on the edge of the bed, looking at her as if she might detonate at any moment, holding an enormous wedge of fluffy white tissue against her face. There was a roll of toilet paper in his free hand. Clearly, he had come prepared.

She tried to say, *I'm not letting you wipe up my bloody snot*, but when she opened her mouth all she got was a gob full of tissue.

"Blow," he repeated sternly.

She blew. She glared at him something fierce, but, well— she still blew.

Absolutely mortifying.

He looked satisfied. Meanwhile, Laura was so embarrassed by the trumpeting sound her nose emitted, she would've happily crawled into a black hole right then and there.

He replaced the snotty tissue with another clump, moving with the speed and efficiency of those mothers on TV—the ones who actually gave a shit about their kids and had developed Mary Poppins-esque superpowers. The kind of mother Laura secretly wanted to be, and not-so-secretly doubted she ever *could* be.

But the sight of Samir right now, the grim determination on his face mingled with tender concern, was making her think that perhaps the superpowers were simply a matter of trying.

She blew again, and he gave her a pleased sort of nod. Then he produced more tissue and began dabbing gently at her cheeks, her eyes, her chin, her neck—Jesus, those tears got around.

But by the time he finished, she felt much drier and less, well, hysterical. Her devastation was more flat and empty, now, rather than an all-consuming, drowning sort of wave.

Laura wasn't sure which of the two states she preferred.

Samir disposed of the tissue and disappeared without a word. She meant to do something useful while he was gone, like pull herself together, but those words snatched up her thoughts again—*"I don't believe you."*

And then all of a sudden, she'd replayed them a thousand times while staring at the polka dots on her pyjama bottoms, and Samir was back with two glasses of water and a bowl, all balanced on one tray.

He put the tray down on the bedside table, handed her one of the glasses, and said, "Drink."

She drank.

He took the empty glass and gave her the bowl. Laura looked down to find a mountain of dry Rice Crispies staring up at her.

She looked up again. "How did you know I—?"

"I pay attention. Eat it."

Her tongue slid out over dry lips. "I... I'm not sure if I can."

He sighed. This was the part where he told her what an awful disappointment she was, right? And she didn't even have the strength to be angry about it, because at that moment, she felt as if it was deserved.

But he didn't say anything of the sort. Instead, he put the bowl back on the tray and said, "Later, then."

She nodded. Bit her lip. Barely felt the sting. After several heavy seconds passed, she managed to force out the words: "Did you hear?"

A shadow passed over his face. "Let's not talk right now. You should sleep. Will you do that for me?"

"Will I... sleep?" Her brain felt as if it was moving more slowly than usual. Sluggish; that was the word. She didn't mind. The slower her brain was, the less her sister's voice could replay in her head.

In fact, she hadn't heard her sister's voice at all, while she was talking to Samir.

"Yes, angel," he said. "Sleep. Please?"

Sleep would be nice. If she could manage it. If her mind would shut up. Laura looked down at her hands, which seemed suddenly small and pathetic. "Will you stay?"

He shouldn't have heard her. She was so quiet, she barely heard herself. But the way he stiffened, the way every inch of him became suddenly alert, and yet contained, she knew that he had.

Still, a taught heartbeat passed before he replied. "Stay here?"

"With me." Shame, her closest friend, had suddenly gone missing. The contrary bitch was probably off sunning itself in Martinique while Laura remained here in rainy old Norfolk, acting a fucking fool.

But then Samir said, "Of course I'll stay. Whatever you want. I'll do whatever you want."

And that would've been good enough, but he did something even better. He pushed her gently back against the pillows, pulled the covers over her and tucked her in. Then he lay beside her, on top of the blankets. He gathered her up against his chest, his arm cradling her belly carefully, her head tucked under his chin. Comfort warmed her aching bones like hot soup on a cold day. He said, "Sleep."

Laura decided that shame could stay on its holiday for as long as it liked.

Then she slept.

CHAPTER THIRTEEN

FOR THE NEXT THREE NIGHTS, Samir slept in Laura's bed.

They didn't discuss it. He wasn't even sure how he'd fallen asleep that first night. He hadn't meant to. He couldn't leave her—not after the snatches of conversation he'd heard as he came into her room, as he put on the clothes she'd left for him. Not when he'd heard her sob, "*Hayley.*" As if something inside her had cracked. Smashed. To pieces.

He still had no idea what, exactly, had happened; he just knew he could never have left her.

But he really hadn't meant to fall asleep.

He hadn't meant to wake her, either, in the early hours of the following morning, when he'd grabbed his salt-water soaked phone and wallet and pressed a kiss to her sleeping cheek. But she'd woken up anyway. She hadn't said a word. She'd simply looked at him with eyes like a stormy sky.

And he'd said without prompting, without a second thought, "I'll be back tonight."

On the fourth day, he locked up the cafe, got in his car, and drove to Laura's—as was becoming his routine. He'd barely stepped foot in his flat above Bianchi's, except to pick up clothes and other shit he'd needed. She always left the front door unlocked for him, and when he entered the house he was greeted by the scent of oddly familiar spices. "Laura?" he called, kicking off his shoes and hanging up his jacket. The fledgling summer had, to the surprise of no-one, turned sour. Ah, Great Britain.

"Kitchen," she called back, sounding almost like her old self. So close to her usual calm, he might've thought she was okay.

If he hadn't known her so well.

But she was still cheerful enough to make him smile, to fill his heart with simple happiness. Laura in a good mood put Samir in a good mood. Laura the way she'd been these past few days made Samir want to hunt down and brutally murder everyone who'd ever hurt her.

Not that he'd actually do such a thing, of course. He couldn't help her sleep every night if he was behind bars, now, could he?

He found her standing over the oven wearing a huge, fluffy jumper, stirring a pot of something that smelled suspiciously like—

"Is that harira?" he asked, incredulous.

That sweet flush spread up her throat. "Yes. Hopefully."

"Hopefully?"

"Well, I tried."

He peered into the pot of rich, spicy soup, spotting chunks of lamb and fat chickpeas. "From the smell of things, you succeeded."

"Oh, don't say that," she muttered. "You'll jinx it."

Samir's hands moved to her hips as he hovered behind her. It was automatic, now—he touched her before even thinking about it, maybe because he spent every night holding her. And yet, despite how natural it felt, a thrill still shot through him at the contact every time. A pulsing awareness that seemed at odds with the sweet, warm comfort she brought him.

He ignored it, of course. He ignored it completely, with great, *great* effort.

"Don't think I'm not happy about it," he said, "but why are you making this?"

She relaxed into his touch, leaning slightly against him. He knew her back hurt, and probably her feet. He wished, sometimes, that she would lean on him completely—but she wouldn't.

Or rather, she hadn't yet. He held out hope that she might, eventually.

They were so close in height that when she turned to look at him, there was barely a breath between them. And yet, she spoke as if they weren't inches away from a kiss. As if the air hadn't grown thick and heavy and ripe around them in an instant.

This was how they were now. It was safe, and it was good. It was what she wanted.

"I made it for you," she said.

Which made sense. It was the obvious conclusion to draw. Laura Albright was making a Moroccan soup, one that she'd first come across in *his* house, years ago, and one that happened to be his favourite. Obviously, she'd made it for him.

And yet, the very idea was so *brilliant*—brighter than the sun, too difficult to look at head-on. Samir cleared his throat to rid it of all the pesky adoration that threatened to spill out. He couldn't get on his knees and pledge eternal devotion because she'd made his favourite fucking soup.

Of course, if he *did* pledge eternal devotion it would be because she was Laura, so different and yet the same, so fragile but steel-hard and ice cold, so lonely and so determinedly alone.

But she wouldn't know that. She'd think it was the soup.

"I wanted to thank you," she said. "I've been... a bit much, the past few days. I know that."

He stiffened. "No, you haven't."

"Well—"

"What does that even mean? A bit much? You're already everything."

She turned then, facing him properly with a little frown. She looked confused, perplexed. "Everything?"

He hadn't really meant to say that, but he wasn't about to take it back. "Laura, you don't—please don't thank me. Don't thank me for the last few days, don't thank me for anything between us. Not ever. When I say it's my pleasure —you don't even understand how much I mean that."

She pressed her lips together. "I was going to tell you... I mean, I was thinking we should talk."

"About?"

She looked away. "I don't know. This. Us."

He was torn between elation at the word *us* and devastation at the way she'd said it. The emotions flew off in different directions, threatening to rip him in two, until all at once, Samir decided. All the mixed-up thoughts and feelings and deep, insistent *needs* she'd dragged from him over the last few months finally came together. The truth sank into his thick skull as if some magician somewhere had snapped his fingers and let the fog clear.

Samir knew, without a shadow of a doubt, exactly what he wanted and how he wanted it.

His hands rose to cradle her cheeks, always so sweet and soft and ready to smile, even when her eyes seemed heavy with despair. They weren't heavy right now. They were wide and confused, almost silvery. His thumbs swept over her skin, memorising its texture.

"Listen," he began. His voice was so low it almost disappeared beneath the echo of rain against the roof. "I don't know what you think we need to talk about, but there's something I want to say first."

"Samir," she whispered. "You're going to complicate things."

"Good. I want to complicate things with you. I want us tied together in a knot so indecipherable, people look at us and can't imagine how we'd ever come apart."

She bit her lip. "You don't—there are a lot of things I haven't told you."

"So tell me. Tell me everything. I'll still be yours."

"Oh, God, don't say that."

"Why not?"

She seemed to be searching frantically for a response, her mouth working. "I—I'm pregnant!"

He laughed. "You're adorable."

"This isn't funny!"

"Sorry, sorry." He schooled his expression into something approaching gravity. "Okay, so. You're pregnant. Does that bother you?"

She flushed. "Does it bother *me?*"

"Do you want to be single right now?"

"I…" She hesitated. He'd kind of sprung this on her, hadn't he? Only it didn't *feel* like that. It felt like something that had been growing underground, a bulb unfurling throughout the seasons until it finally sprouted and bloomed.

"You know you can tell me the truth," he said softly. "You don't have to keep me happy. There are no consequences with me."

Something in her seemed to relax. That was both satisfying and infuriating, because it only confirmed what he'd long suspected. But he wasn't going to think about that—about the man in her past—right now. All he could focus on was her face, and the play of emotions flitting through her eyes like shadows over still water.

Finally, she whispered, "I did want to be single. Not just single—I wanted to be alone. I felt… I felt like I didn't know myself anymore. Like I needed to get back to *me* again, so I could be better in time for…" She nodded down between their bodies, to the swell of her stomach. And, yeah, he knew. Better than she'd expect. Better than *he'd* ever expected.

He'd been feeling a similar urge, recently, to become the best man he could be.

"So I did want to be single." She sucked in a shaking breath. "I just didn't expect to find someone who'd make me feel more like myself than I have in years."

His pleasure was hot and golden, shot through with a

silvery promise that was just like her eyes. Her gaze was always so cool, but right now it felt molten. "Laura," he murmured, "I want to be with you. And I know you have a lot more to risk than I do, but I wouldn't say it if I wasn't all in. I love you." Now he'd said the words, he wondered how he'd ever managed to keep them in.

She squeezed her eyes shut—but not fast enough to stop a tear escaping, gliding down her cheek silently.

"Oh, angel, don't cry." Samir's heart squeezed even as he bent his head to kiss the tear away. "Please don't cry. I'm telling you because you should know, not because I need anything from you. I'm saying this because it's true. I don't want a thing in return."

"I know you don't," she choked out. "I just—I don't—you shouldn't—"

"Shh. Let's make a deal, okay? You don't tell me I can't love you, or I don't love you, or I shouldn't love you—"

"But I have so much—"

"Or that I can't love the baby—"

Her eyes flew open. "You—?"

"Of course I love the baby. That's why I've been working so hard to protect them from your horrible taste in names."

She snorted out a laugh, then clapped a hand over her mouth. But as soon as her eyes met his, her embarrassment melted back into amusement. She laughed again.

She didn't stop herself this time.

"So," he said smugly as she giggled. "You don't tell me who I can and can't love, and in return…"

"Yes?" she asked innocently. "In return, what?"

Because she knew, the minx, that he hadn't thought his

bargain through. But he managed to think on his feet. "In return, I'll put something Italian on the menu at Bianchi's."

She narrowed her eyes, considering. "Pizza. It has to be pizza."

"Seriously? You want me to sell pizza at a cafe?"

"I said what I said." She arched a brow.

"Fine! Pizza it is. Deal?"

A slow smile spread across her face as she said, "Deal."

In that moment, with splotches of pink blooming across her tear-stained skin, and hesitant happiness lighting her up, she was the most beautiful thing he'd ever seen. His chest hurt. Apparently, being hopelessly in love kind of felt like a heart attack.

God, Hassan was going to be so fucking smug about this. Although he'd been wrong about one thing: the way Samir loved Laura was nothing like the teenage adoration and attraction between them, no matter how deep that bond had been.

The way Samir loved Laura right now was deeper than anything he'd ever felt.

CHAPTER FOURTEEN

THE SOUND of Samir brushing his teeth in the en-suite was both reassuring and terrifying.

Over the past few nights, Laura's subconscious had come to associate that sound with a long, peaceful, dreamless sleep. The feel of Samir's broad chest against her back, his slow, heavy breaths over her hair, his big hand resting on her belly like a shield, had become her anchor. But now...

Now, Samir *thought* he loved her. When he'd said it, her heart had cartwheeled around in her chest for a second. Then it had put its back out, twisted an ankle, and remembered that it was a fragile, useless, battered old thing for a reason.

When Samir came out of the bathroom, she'd have to tell him. Everything. And not just because he deserved honesty —not just because a lie, even a lie of omission, would be like taking his trust and drowning it.

She had to tell him because she loved him.

"You seem serious." He stood in the bathroom's narrow doorway, looking obnoxiously handsome and alarmingly broad. As usual. The sight of his slow, easy grin had her heart pounding; add in his bare chest and it was a wonder she hadn't collapsed yet. Really, half-nakedness was highly irresponsible, coming from a man who looked like that.

"We need to talk," she said, then wanted to take it back immediately. *We need to talk?* Could she be anymore obliquely ominous? "I mean—I'd like us to... have... a chat." She pushed her hair behind her ears, except there was nothing to push because she'd braided it up for bed. So she ended up kind of... uselessly stroking her own face.

Cool, Laura. Very cool.

He raised his brows as he came toward her. "Is this about your addiction to deep conditioner? Because it's okay. I already know. I snooped through your bathroom cabinet two days ago."

She was trying so hard to be mature, and he ruined it without effort. Even as she resented her own helpless snort of laughter, she loved him. So much. Probably too much.

Definitely too much, since he'd be gone within the hour.

"Sit down," she said, and he sat. Fuck, she wished they weren't doing this now, but it had taken her all night to gather up what scraps of courage she had left. She felt a little safer, curled up under the blankets, but that comfort was undermined by the sight of him shirtless in her bed, wearing those clingy pyjama bottoms that, in her opinion, showed far too much of the shape of his thighs...

Not that she was necessarily complaining.

Focus!

He was looking at her with gentle interest, but not an

ounce of worry. He wasn't bracing himself for a hit, for the sting of betrayal. He should be.

"I'm still married," she blurted out.

Ah. There it was. His face slackened for a minute, mouth falling open, those sharp brows twitching as if he was too shocked to actually raise them. After a heavy pause, he said, "*Married?*"

Laura's throat was tight. Her skin was stretched too thin, hot and prickling with shame. She looked down at her lap and found her hands twisting anxiously together, her fingers red and white like candy cane. "Yes," she whispered.

"To Daniel." Samir's tone was suddenly flat, devoid of the swell of emotion that made him *him*. No matter how he felt, it was always right there in his voice, his eyes, his actions, for anyone to see.

But not right now, apparently.

That was a bad sign, wasn't it? Not just a bad sign, her mind supplied—a dangerous one. Laura's clinging hands released each other and crept toward her belly, as if they could do anything against a man Samir's size. And even though it had been months since she'd left Daniel, months since she'd had to do this, her mind fell back into the routine easily: cataloguing paths to the nearest exit, considering what to say that might talk him down or distract him or appease him—

"Jesus, Laura, breathe. I'm not—" Samir's hand rose, and she couldn't help it—she jerked away, so fast and so hard she almost fell off the bed.

But he grabbed her, wrapping an arm around her hips, dragging her back. Toward him.

"Angel, I'm not mad at you. You know that, don't you?"

He pulled her into his lap as if she were a child and took her face in his hands, frowning down at her. "*Laura*. Please. Breathe. You're worrying me."

Her brain seemed to be delayed, panicking too hard to process instantly, but the words finally sank in. She was holding her breath. As soon as she became conscious of it, the tight scream of her lungs went from unnoticed to unbearable, and Laura exhaled on a gasp.

As she sucked down oxygen, Samir's hand circled her back, slow and soothing. Which didn't make any sense. He wasn't supposed to be touching her, helping her, caring for her—

But then the last of Laura's instinctive panic faded, and she remembered that this was Samir. Not Daniel. Not even *remotely* Daniel. Samir wasn't going to hurt her. He could hate her fucking guts and he still wouldn't hurt her. He didn't want any harm to come to her, and especially not to the baby.

"You okay?" he asked softly. His other hand closed around her wrist, his thumb stroking back and forth, flutters of sensation gliding over her raw nerves. She wished he wouldn't be like this. She wished he wouldn't be so gentle, wouldn't make her feel so safe, even as he prepared to leave her.

Because he was going to leave her, no matter what he said. She'd seen it in his face. He was horrified.

Samir brought a hand to her chin and pushed, making her meet his eyes. His beautiful, impossible, midnight-ocean eyes. "Hey," he murmured. "Speak to me."

Through sheer force of will, Laura managed to sound

passably calm. "I'm fine. You can... put me down, or whatever."

His lips tilted slightly. "Actually, if you don't mind, I think I'll keep hold of you."

She blinked rapidly. And then, in a sparkling display of intelligence, said: "Um. What?"

He settled back against the cushions, drawing her closer to his chest. "This sounds like a conversation that's going to piss me off. Holding on to you keeps me calm. Please, continue."

"Con...tinue?"

"Yeah. With the talking. Say something else. Like, I don't know—*I'm married to Daniel, but he died in a mysterious boating accident last week.* Like that."

Ah. Laura gave a heavy sigh. "He's not dead."

"That's a shame."

She shouldn't laugh. This was a very serious conversation. But she had to smile a little bit. She couldn't help it.

"So what you're telling me," Samir said, "is that Daniel—the man who won't take responsibility for his own kid, the man who left you—"

"I left *him*," Laura interrupted, because apparently she still had her pride.

"Sorry," he said wryly. If she didn't know any better, she'd think that was a smile she heard in his voice. But she couldn't see, because he was holding her head quite firmly against his chest. She could hear his heart beating, way faster than it should, and feel the rumble of his deep voice. "The man *you* left," he amended. "The man you're fucking terrified of—"

"I—I'm not—" She wanted to say, *I'm not terrified of him.* But then she remembered she wasn't supposed to be lying.

After a little pause, Samir said grimly, "Right. Him. That guy. That Daniel. You're telling me that he's your *husband?*"

He was angry, but trying to hide it—or at least tone it down. She felt it anyway, because she felt *him*, too intense to miss. It almost made her nervous.

And yet, the soothing stroke of his thumb over her arm was so... relaxing. When she managed to choke out, "Yes," she sounded as if she were trapped halfway between anxiety and exhaustion. Which wasn't entirely inaccurate. Although the anxiety part was fading with each passing second.

"He married you," Samir said flatly. "He married you, and promised to love you and cherish you, and then you got pregnant and he..."

"Punched a wall," she supplied. "And told me to get an abortion."

She felt every inch of the deep, shaking breath Samir took. When his chest expanded, she felt it. When he heaved out a sigh, she felt it. When his hand, which had been stroking her hair slowly, faltered, she felt it.

And slowly began to understand what it meant.

Finally, he said, "Okay. Okay. So you're married." A pause. "You didn't tell me that."

"I know," she said, trying to sit up. "I know—"

"Don't," he murmured, pulling her back against his chest. "Stay here. Please."

"Okay," she said, as if she were doing him a favour. As if the fact that he apparently needed her wasn't sweet enough to make her heart sing. His chest hair tickled her cheek, the skin beneath it reassuringly warm, his arms solid around her. The way he held her was impossibly *good*—as if she could leave, if she wanted, but he really fucking hoped she wouldn't.

She didn't.

"I know," she repeated. "I should have said something. I understand if you—if you can't..." She couldn't even say the words.

But Samir had never had a problem filling her silences. "Right. Well, no disrespect to the great institution of marriage, but I really do not give a fuck."

Laura's mind blanked. "You don't?"

She felt his massive shoulders shift as he shrugged. "Marriage is a promise. Yes, it's a whole legal thing, but the important part is the promise. You make vows for a reason. He broke them. What I do care about is you." His voice, always so confident, became slower, more careful. "You've been here a while now, love. But you're not divorced."

"Yet," she said quickly. "I filed for divorce in March."

"March? It's almost July."

"I know. He won't cooperate. I mean, he won't sign the petition to acknowledge he received it, so I have to go to court and convince them he's in contempt, and it's this whole fucked-up thing..."

"Okay," he said. "But you don't still want to be with him?"

"*No.*" The word was ripped from her chest with enough vehemence to alarm even herself. She cleared her throat. "Sorry. No. God, I fucking hate him. If you knew him, you'd—"

"I don't need to know him," Samir said mildly. "Ten

minutes ago, I tried to touch you and you flinched so hard you almost fell off the bed. I already hate him, Laura."

She swallowed. "The other day… the first night you stayed. I was on the phone with my sister."

For the first time, Samir pulled back a little bit—enough to see her face. To look her in the eyes. "What did she say?" he asked gently.

Laura's reply was a whisper. "She said she didn't believe me."

He didn't ask questions. He didn't ask what, exactly, Hayley didn't believe. He didn't press for details or explanations or emotions she was too tired to give.

Instead, he said simply, "*I* believe you." And she was flooded with a relief so intense, it was almost painful.

Then came the impulse to speak. Finally, to speak, and never ever stop.

SHE TOLD HIM EVERYTHING.

About the woman this Daniel fucker had been with for years—the mysterious Ruth—without anyone in Ravenswood even knowing. About the way he'd used her, used both of them, before turning Laura and everyone else against his 'other woman'.

Even about the things he said and done. The poison he'd dripped into Laura's ear during the years of their relationship. About how no-one could love her but him, about how she was nothing without him, about the way she looked and spoke and smiled until she didn't know how to *be* without his approval.

Apparently, he didn't offer that approval often.

Samir laid there with the woman he loved in his arms, and listened to the halting, desperate tale spilling from her lips like sour juice from the too-tight skin of rotting fruit. He didn't flinch when she quoted her so-called-husband in a voice as flat and dead as driftwood. *"You don't need to work, Laura. You know you're too stupid for that anyway. Whose dick did you have to suck to get that degree? If it weren't for me watching you, you'd be a drunken whore like your mother. You're lucky I want to fuck you at all, looking like that. You should be grateful."*

He didn't falter when she described the secret ways her husband had hurt her. The way he ripped out single strands of her hair, one by one. The way he held her down. The way he covered her nose and mouth until she couldn't breathe, because he liked to watch her panic.

He didn't punch the fucking wall when she told him about the night she'd finally managed to leave, or the fact that she'd run to Daniel's father rather than her own family because *they* refused to hear a word against the town's sweetheart.

He couldn't punch a wall ever again, actually. He couldn't even slice up onions like a madman. He could never come close to losing his temper, Samir decided, because he would rather die, boiled alive from the inside out by pent-up rage, than ever do anything to make Laura flinch, or hesitate, or remember.

When she ran out of words, she kissed him. It was only the soft brush of her lips against his, tasting like salt, that made him realise he was crying too. She shouldn't have been the one to brush away his tears, but she did. Then she kissed him again. They lay for a while, face to face, lips grazing lips in petal-soft whispers. She'd kiss him. He'd kiss her. She'd kiss him. And then one of her rigid joints would unlock and she'd do something that made his chest tighten, like touch his cheek, or run her fingers through his hair, or just hold on to him for a moment, a heartbeat. And then he'd kiss her. And she'd kiss him.

He didn't know how long they'd been there, in their own reality, when she tried and failed to stifle a yawn against his mouth. That familiar, rosy flush crept over her chest as she looked away and mumbled, "Sorry."

He smiled. "*I'm* sorry. I shouldn't be keeping you up."

"You're not keeping me up." Then, her voice almost a whisper: "You're the only thing that gets me to sleep."

He pressed his forehead to hers, shut his eyes, and breathed in the scent of her—clean hair and tear-stained skin and the ghost of the ocean, and the thing beneath it all that was pure Laura, the thing that felt like home and a holiday combined. He didn't mention his strong suspicion that he'd no longer be able to sleep without the feel of her tucked close to his chest, or the swell of her stomach beneath his hand. Instead, he said, "How do you not need to pee right now?"

"I *do* need to pee right now."

He huffed out a laugh. "Go on, then."

"Don't tell me to go! I know when to go."

"So why aren't you going?"

She sat up with a snort and a flick of her long, thick, braid, giving him the evil eye. He tried to look subdued, as opposed to amused and adoring. The jury was out on how well he did, since whatever she saw on his face made her scoff and smile all at once.

He lay in bed while she went to the bathroom for the thousandth time that day. When she returned, they settled into position without a word, as if they'd been doing this forever: her back against his chest, his arm secure around her. But this time, he was beneath the blankets with her, instead of lying on top of them. This time, their feet tangled together, and his knee slid between her thighs. She sighed and wiggled her hips as if that was just right, and then she found his hand on her belly and laced her fingers through his. He counted about thirty seconds before her breathing fell into the familiar, soothing rhythm of sleep.

It took Samir a hell of a lot longer, but he got there in the end.

He dreamt of her.

CHAPTER FIFTEEN

Laura sat on the toilet, bleary-eyed and more than a little annoyed, as the rising sun spilled its pale glow into the en-suite. Somehow, she had woken up with a desperately full bladder and a mouth drier than stale bread, probably because of last night's crying. Plus, her back ached even though she'd spent the last six hours lying down.

Ah, the joys of pregnancy.

But she wouldn't be pregnant much longer, would she? The thought gripped her and refused to let go, impatience and excitement intertwining. She looked down at her belly and whispered, "Hurry up, okay? I want to see you."

Bump didn't reply, but she flattered herself that they wanted to see her, too.

Laura washed her hands, downed the bottle of water on the counter, and wandered—or waddled, really—back into the bedroom with a smile on her face. Then stopped in her tracks as she saw Samir.

He hadn't stirred when she'd eased out of his arms five

minutes ago, but he was awake now. He sat up in bed, his thick hair pointing in ten different directions, the white sheets bright against his bare, brown chest. He had a bottle of water in his hand and a sleepy smile on his face. "Thirsty?"

Oh, she loved that smile. His happiness made her happy. His grins left her content. His laughter lifted her. Every time. "I drank the one you left in the bathroom. Good move, by the way."

"Hydration is very important as you approach the third trimester," he said gravely, before downing half the bottle in one go.

"Is it, now?" Her midwife *had* said that at their last appointment, but Samir hadn't been there.

He'd been waiting in the car.

"Yeah. It's in my book."

She came over to the bed, sinking down with a wince. Her joints always ached in the mornings. "Your book?"

"My baby book." He lay down and drew her back into his chest, just as they'd slept last night, legs tangled together. "*Bump and Beyond.* I bought it online."

"Um... what?" It was an odd sensation, being caught between laughter and tears. Good tears, but still tears. "You bought *Bump and Beyond*?"

"Uh, yeah. Did you think I just knew all that baby stuff? I'm good, but I'm not that good."

Ah. So that was how he'd magically known, over the past few weeks, all those things he'd mentioned in passing about blood pressure, and iron levels, and vitamin K. It had never occurred to her that he might actually go out of his way to learn.

For her.

She turned as best she could, considering one of his legs was wedged between hers and the weight of his arm was wrapped firmly around her body. He moved back a little to accommodate her shift, and she was able to meet his eyes without dislodging their position. She would hate to do that, after all. She really, really liked their position.

"You got a book," she said. As if they hadn't already established that fact.

"Of course. How else was I supposed to know what's going on with you? You never let me come to your appointments."

"I thought it would be weird," she mumbled. "Like, pushy, or—"

"Nope." He kissed her cheek. "I told you I was going to look after you. I told you that right from the start."

She frowned. "Wait—when did you get the book?"

"I don't know..." His brow furrowed as he thought back. "April, I suppose."

"*April?*"

"Yeah." He kissed her cheek again, lower this time—her jaw, really. Soft and slow, and careful. Something about how deliberate it was shot through her like lightning through the clouds. "You're not upset, are you?"

Upset that he cared enough, even then, to buy himself a pregnancy guide? Upset that he hadn't mentioned it for months, as if it didn't even matter, as if it didn't mean the world? Upset that he was there, that he was with her, that he *loved* her?

"No," she breathed. "I'm not upset. I just remembered something, though."

"Yeah?"

"You... last night, you said you loved me."

"I did," he murmured. He pressed a kiss to her throat, just below her ear, gentle but lingering. "I do," he said, his lips brushing her skin as he formed the words, still so close. "I love you. I love everything about you. I love the way you smile at me like I'm the only person in the room. I love the way you just *do* things—even when you're afraid, so afraid I can see it around you like a shadow. I love how you laugh with the old ladies at the cafe even when their jokes aren't funny. I love the way your face lights up when you talk about your friends. I love it when you come out with these blunt, bitchy comments sometimes, then look at me like you hope I didn't notice."

"Oh my God," she groaned, the soaring delight in her chest sagging a little. "You noticed? You noticed that I'm evil?"

"I noticed that you're *funny*," he said wryly. "And, yeah, a little bit evil. All the best people are."

Laura huffed out a laugh. "If you say so."

"I do say so." He kissed her throat, and she didn't mean to, but *fuck*—she released a sigh that was mostly a moan, low and broken and lustful enough to make her blush. He tensed for a second—she *felt* it—and then his hand trailed down to the narrow strip of skin her T-shirt couldn't quite cover, right above her waistband. His fingertips barely glided over her abdomen, tracing slow, lazy circles that made her shiver. "You okay?" he asked.

"Yes," she gasped, completely unconvincing.

"You sure?" His mouth moved to her ear, and she could

feel the slow curve of his smile. "Whatever you need, angel. That's what I'm here for."

"I…" She wanted to say she loved him. Because she did, suddenly and undeniably, so much that she *had* to tell him.

But she couldn't.

Something lodged itself in her throat, something bigger than fear, greater than terror, and her heart fell. Surely, she was brave enough. Surely nothing, no-one, could stop her from telling Samir exactly what he meant to her.

But it seemed that something could. She wasn't brave at all.

"Hey," he said, his voice gentler now. "You're thinking again."

She laughed, in spite of everything. "Thinking is generally considered a good thing."

"Nah. Not if it makes you look like that."

"Like what?"

"Lost. Can I kiss you, angel?"

Just like that, the tension between them, cotton-thick and satin soft, returned. It was delicious. It was divine. It was easy, all of a sudden, to forget her disappointment in herself. "Yes," she whispered, her eyes meeting his, the moon and the night sky coming together. Where they belonged.

"Would you say no?" he asked. His fingers traced that barely-there pattern against her taut skin, pushing her heart rate up with each lazy swirl. "If you didn't want me to? Would you tell me?"

"I would. I'm not afraid of you."

She saw a flare of satisfaction in his eyes. "Good. Don't ever be afraid of me, Laura. I'm yours."

The press of his lips against hers was achingly tender,

painfully sweet. His tongue feathered over her own as if he was testing the waters. As if he was learning her.

So she kissed him back, hot and hard enough to make her feelings clear. Her reward was the deep, heady groan that rumbled through his chest—and the thick curve of his erection against her side. She'd felt that hardness before, when he forgot to keep his hips canted away from hers. Now, with their bodies intertwined and nothing between them, there was no hiding it. And when she arched into the sweet pressure of his cock, Samir deepened the kiss, his hand snaking up her body, under her T-shirt.

He found her tits, heavy and unconfined, giving one a barely-there squeeze. She moaned in frustration as his mouth left hers. "Perfect," he murmured. "So perfect." His thumb circled her nipple until her breaths came fast and laboured. "Does it hurt, love?" he asked. But his heavy-lidded gaze was dark and knowing, a smile teasing his full lips. "You're so sensitive. Do you want me to stop?"

"No," she gasped, squirming against him. She needed to arch into his touch, needed to thrust herself back so his cock would rub against her *just* right—and *fuck*, she couldn't do both, and she felt so hot and wet between her legs—

He dragged up her T-shirt completely, without warning, shocking a gasp out of her. "Maybe if I kiss it better," he said, as he exposed her bare breasts to the air. "Would you like that? Oh, fuck, Laura, you're so lovely."

She held her breath as his face slackened, as the teasing glint left his eye and his lips parted. He stared down at her swollen, stretch-marked belly as if it were dessert. His gaze settled on her tender, reddened breasts, the stretch-marks even brighter than they were on her stomach—and his cheeks flushed darker, his teeth sinking into his lower lip.

"Jesus," he groaned. "God. You are so fucking sexy."

She'd expected him to say something sweet and complimentary because he was that kind of man. She'd expected to thank him with a blush while believing not a single word of it.

He was destroying her expectations.

His words sent heat tearing through her, less a flush of embarrassment and more a raging forest fire of answering desire. Because he most definitely desired her. She believed it beyond the feel of his hardness or the words on his lips. She believed it because his hands were shaking, and because he bent his head over her chest with a noise that sounded like a growl, and because he sucked her nipple into his mouth almost hungrily, his hips grinding against her in time with every tight pull.

"Oh my God Samir no wait yes keep—" Laura's words spilled out without permission or restraint or sense, and she couldn't have stopped herself if she'd tried. Her hands seemed to have a mind of their own, running over his bare skin, tracing the coarse path of his chest hair all the way down, and over his abs, and then to his waistband.

And she didn't stop there. She felt distantly scandalised but achingly, desperately thirsty as she shoved his pyjama bottoms down. Not all the way down—that required sensible, conscious thought about how clothes were supposed to be treated. No; Laura shoved them down to mid-thigh before fisting his cock.

He grunted, his face buried against her breasts as his hips jerked, that thick, hot dick thrusting into her palm. He felt so unbelievable, hard and way too *real,* and when she ran her thumb over the silken head it came away slick with pre-come. She could feel her pulse pounding through her clit, and her thighs were slippery with her own wetness, and she had this unbelievably strong urge to spread her legs wide and guide him inside her.

She hadn't felt that urge in years. Fucking years.

"Samir," she gasped. Her breath hitched as his hand found her arse, kneading greedily, almost as if he *wanted* just as much as she did.

He looked up, his mouth lush and swollen, leaving her breast cool and tingling. "Tell me. What do you need?"

"I…" She blushed, suddenly realising that she hadn't said anything like this in forever. She didn't know *how* to say it anymore. But then she remembered a night on the beach fifteen years ago, and she found her courage as she borrowed the words of her younger self. "I think we should do that thing."

She knew he remembered because a grin cut through the arousal on his face, and he said, just like he had back then: "*That thing?*"

"You know," she murmured, her lips twitching.

"Yeah," he said dryly. "I know." But then his expression sobered. "I'm sorry, love, but I don't think I…." Just as her heart began to fall, his smile returned. "Hold on a sec."

He pulled away, and without the heat of his body she felt suddenly exposed. More naked—or half-naked—than she had been seconds before. But she resisted the urge to examine her flaws in the sunlight streaming through the curtains. *He thinks you look fine. He thinks you look sexy.*

Laura ran an absent finger over the brown line bisecting her belly and decided that he was right.

Then Samir muttered, "Oh, thank fuck." She turned in time to see him pull a condom from one of the many little pockets in his wallet. He squinted at the back of the foil for a second before giving her a teasing smile. "Alright, angel. We'll do that thing."

He knelt beside her on the bed, his thighs thick and muscled, his cock jutting dark and heavy between them, the fat head gleaming. He looked obscene. He looked delicious. When he put the condom aside instead of tearing it open, Laura wanted to pout like a spoiled brat.

But then he pulled her fully onto her back before easing off the last of her clothes. And *then* he slid his palms up her legs, past her swollen ankles and her aching calves, until he reached her sensitive inner thighs.

"Do you get wet like this every night?" he murmured, his fingers gliding over her skin. "So wet you make a mess of yourself? Because I've been feeling guilty, Laura, so damn guilty about how hard you make me..." He spread her wide and lowered his head until she could feel his cool breath against her fevered pussy. She was going to say something. She was going to try, at least. But then the broad, wet flat of his tongue slid over her, parting her folds further, massaging her with each languorous stroke, and all she could manage was a high, broken cry that made her slap a hand over her mouth.

His fingers dug into her thighs, holding them open when she would've slammed them shut. He dipped his tongue into her entrance, lapping up her juices in a wet, warm rhythm that might've been soothing if it hadn't turned the blood in her veins to lava. And things only got worse when he replaced his tongue with his fingers, easing those thick digits inside her, his knuckles brushing a spot that almost made her leap out of her skin.

"God, you feel good," he muttered, his breath coming in pants. "Gonna feel so fucking amazing on my dick..."

The words made her imagine that delicious stretch between her legs intensifying, made her dream up the feel of that thick, hard length pushing into her. And then his tongue found her clit, tracing slow, easy circles around the swollen nub, and every time he got to the left side her legs spasmed and wild pleasure bloomed, and fuck, he must have noticed, because he started licking *just* the left side, rubbing her with his tongue and stroking her tightening pussy until she couldn't think, couldn't breathe, couldn't—couldn't—

The long, low moan she released was as uncontrollable as the mind-numbing bliss spiralling through her body. Laura came so hard, she almost forgot where she was.

While she caught her breath and gathered her wits, she was distantly aware of him moving. Of the slick sound of a condom being rolled on, and then his warmth beside her again. Her limbs felt like liquid as he moved her, pushing her onto her side, pulling her into his chest the way they lay every night as they fell asleep. But they weren't falling asleep now. He pressed hot kisses to her throat, and Laura's lust returned way quicker than her senses. She arched back against him, and without clothes between them his condom-clad cock slid over her pussy.

"Ohhh, God," she moaned, rolling her hips again. "Samir. Fuck me fuck me fuck me—"

His hand caught her leg just above the knee, and then he

parted her thighs, pushing her bent leg high. He pressed his lips against her jaw, his morning stubble grazing her skin. "I want to kiss you when I'm inside you."

She'd never done it like this before, but she supposed she was too big for most positions. And the comforting feel of his chest against her back... *yes*. Yes. This was perfect.

Laura grasped his length and guided him to her pussy, anticipation fizzing through her like champagne bubbles. The blunt tip of his cock nudged its way into her slick channel, and a moan slipped from her lips.

"Look at me," he said, his voice tender and pleading and thick with desire. The hand on her thigh moved as he twisted his hips, giving her more of his dick. She turned her head to look at him as his fingers found her clit. "So beautiful," he murmured, his lips brushing hers, his stroking fingers sending spirals of pleasure through her. "My Laura. My love."

"Samir," she said, reaching back to run a hand through his hair. "I... I—"

"It's okay." He kissed her again, hot and slow, as his hips moved. As he ground into her, rubbing that sensitive place inside, his fingers strummed her swollen clit. "Just love me like this," he whispered against her lips. "Like this."

And she did. When she came again with his name on her lips; when he held her impossibly close as he lost control; when he spilled into the condom with a moan torn from deep inside him.

She did.

CHAPTER SIXTEEN

"Are you sure this omelette will be up to Max's standards?"

Samir leant against the kitchen counter as he whisked a bowl of eggs, trying not to look as besotted as he felt. "You know, Bianchi's is *my* cafe."

"And yet, I've never seen you cook." Laura sat at the worn old table, biting down on a smile, eyes dancing, cheeks flushed. She looked—in a word—satisfied. He liked that look.

He liked satisfying her too. In fact, once she was fed, he'd like to satisfy her again.

"You know I can cook," Samir said, turning back to the oven. It would be harder for lust to overwhelm him if he didn't look at her, right?

"What I know," she said pertly, "is that Max's omelettes have kept me happy for months, but yours are an unknown entity."

Hm. Apparently, the sound of her voice, combined with that attitude, did it for him just as much as the sight of her.

Interesting.

Resigned to his lustful fate, Samir allowed himself the luxury of meeting her eyes again. "Careful. You might hurt my feelings."

She propped her elbows on the table, resting her face in her hands. He tried to avoid the swell of her cleavage, but... well, actually, no he didn't. He didn't try at all. "Oh dear," she murmured archly. "I'd *hate* to hurt your feelings. You—"

Whatever the minx was about to say, it was interrupted by the obnoxiously low, rich rumble of an engine pulling into the driveway. Samir felt his brow crease just as an answering frown appeared on Laura's face.

"Don't get up," he said. "I'll see who it is."

She ignored him, of course, rising with a soft groan and padding after him into the living room, whose curtain-covered bay windows looked out onto the drive. Samir pulled the cream fabric aside to find a huge, blue BMW sitting in the driveway. And then he heard Laura's strangled intake of breath, felt her warmth slip away from him as she retreated.

"Get back," she ordered, her voice clipped. "Now. He'll see you."

He dropped the curtain and turned to face her. "Who?"

But he already knew by the look on her face, by the colour of her skin, grey-toned and bloodless.

"Daniel," she whispered. "Daniel's here."

Fury was such a cold word. Samir hadn't always thought so—in fact, he'd never considered the word at all. Never found himself analysing its sound and texture and taste, or comparing it to the explosiveness of the emotion. But he was doing it right now because he had to concentrate on *something* to keep his sudden, burning anger in check.

Apparently, the knowledge that Daniel was within reach made his throttling hand really itchy.

But he couldn't let Laura see that, not even a hint. So he swallowed down all of his rage and kept his voice calm and steady. "He knew you were here?"

"No," she said, staring, wide-eyed, at the floor. As if searching for something. Her hands were cradled over her belly, her shoulders, always so proud, hunched protectively. "I—I only told Trevor and Hayley..." And then her eyes squeezed shut, heartbreaking resignation on her face. "Hayley. Fuck."

He didn't know how she'd react, but she looked so hopeless, so betrayed, so blindsided—he had to touch her. He approached slowly, at first, and she watched him with confusion on her face. As if she had no idea why he might possibly come toward her with his arms outstretched. As if he hadn't held her against his heart every night since that awful phone call.

But then, when he hugged her close, she relaxed. He could feel her coming alive again, transforming from a cold, petrified creature to something warm and human in his arms. "Don't panic," he whispered. "I've got you."

And then the knock came.

Samir hadn't seen Daniel through the tinted windows of that ridiculous car, but from the sound his fists made against the front door, he was a big fucker. Then came his voice, smug and almost gleeful in its cruelty, a threat creeping through each word on tiger-soft paws.

"Laura. I know you're in there."

Samir pulled back a little, looking down at the woman in his arms. He came face to face with the last thing he'd expected: not terrified tears, but icy determination.

"Laura!" More banging, even louder this time. "Open the fucking door. I have shit to do, you know."

"With me," Samir whispered, his hands sliding into her hair, his eyes catching hers. "You're with me. You're okay."

She nodded, lips pressed into a fine line.

"Tell me what you're thinking," he said. "Tell me what you want to do."

"I'm thinking about Ruth."

"Ruth?"

She gave him a shaking half-smile. "If Ruth were here, she'd go out there and tell him to fuck off."

He traced the slight curve of that smile with his thumb, clinging to it, letting it stave off his worry. "Yeah? So what are we gonna do?"

The smile widened. "We're gonna go out there and tell him to fuck off."

IT WAS ONLY when Samir opened the door that Laura remembered she was still in her pyjamas. She hadn't brushed her hair, and she kind of needed the loo—*again*—and Samir wasn't even wearing a shirt. But it was too late to worry about that, wasn't it? Because now the door was open, and Samir was pushing Daniel back, back, back, giving Laura room...

And now she was outside, in the open, two metres away from her worst fucking nightmare, with Samir standing between them. She hovered in the doorway, her eyes on Samir's broad back instead of the man opposite him. Her husband. Daniel.

God, she was going to *kill* Hayley. How could her sister do this?

"Who the fuck are you?" Daniel was demanding, his voice deeper than usual. He always did that around men who intimidated him. Which meant that Samir intimidated him.

Good.

"I'm Samir Bianchi. Who the fuck are *you*?" She watched as Samir's already broad shoulders seemed to grow wider, as he crossed his arms and settled into his stance like a bodyguard or something.

He would protect her. She'd known that, logically, but suddenly the reality of it filled her up and set her free. She could do this. Daniel couldn't bully her into silence or threaten her into submission because the greatest power he had over her wouldn't work anymore. His physical strength was officially contained.

And without it, what was he, really?

Cunning; that's what. She remembered, her heart sinking like a stone, when he spoke again, his voice softer now. Hesitant, almost hurt, but brave. "I'm Daniel Burne," he said. And then she saw him, saw his face as he searched her out over Samir's shoulder. And he really did look like an innocent man coming to a terrible realisation. "I'm—I'm Laura's husband." His voice cracked a little on that last word. "Laura? Honey? What's going on?"

She swallowed. "Stop it."

"Stop what?" His face sagged, hopeless and wan. "Baby—"

"Don't talk to her," Samir said. He didn't sound uncertain. He didn't sound confused. He didn't even sound defensive.

He sounded bored.

Because Samir, she suddenly remembered, knew that a person could seem honest with every word and breath and beat of their heart, and still be a fucking liar.

She almost fainted with pure relief.

"Listen," Daniel was saying, in his *trying so hard to be reasonable* tone. "I don't know who you are, and I don't know what's going on here, but this is my wife. She's having my baby! You can't stop me talking to her."

Samir gave a weary sigh. "Laura, love?"

Her reply was calm and even, thank God. "Yes?"

"Do you want him to talk to you?"

She swallowed. "No."

Samir shrugged. "Well, there it is." Then he called to her again. "Do you have something to say to him?"

"I do." She came closer, but not too close. Samir was smart enough not to take his eyes off Daniel for a second, but she didn't want to complicate things by putting herself in range of his cruel hands. She moved until she could meet her husband's eyes, twin jewels glittering in his deceptively calm face, promising retribution.

She was not afraid.

Much.

But more importantly, she realised that one day, she really *wouldn't* be afraid. Not at all.

"You can stop pretending," she said. "Or maybe you can't.

I don't know. I've never really understood how your mind works, but I think you really commit to the lies, don't you?" Her mouth twisted into something that felt almost like a smile. "I don't like having you here, so I'll be quick. Whether you sign or not, eventually, we *will* be divorced. And when that happens, you will owe me child maintenance."

Daniel's innocent expression crumbled like dust, replaced by an acid-sharp mix of hatred and disgust. "Is that how you got this poor fucker to sleep with you? Did you promise him *my* money, Laura?"

She watched Samir's hands curl into fists, watched the muscles in his back tense.

"I don't want your money," she said, with complete honesty. "I don't want anything to do with you. I don't want you to be this baby's father—I don't even want your name on the birth certificate. But I will *take* your money if you make me."

"You're a manipulative, conniving bitch." He said it calmly, his expression smoothing into handsome blankness. The sun glinted off his bright hair. It really was a lovely colour. And he really was so pretty, with the eyes and the smile and the jaw. She'd be so very pleased if he fell off the face of the fucking earth.

"I don't know what you're doing with my sister," she said, "but whatever it is, stop. Leave her alone."

Surprise flitted across his face for a second. He hadn't been expecting that. Probably because Daniel had never thought about anyone other than himself in his entire fucking life. He wouldn't expect Laura to.

But he recovered quickly enough, with a burst of laughter. "Is that what this is, honey? Are you jealous?"

She steeled herself against the mocking words, the insinuations that always drove her off-track and into a corner, the way he corralled her so smoothly. "Listen to me. You will leave me alone, you will leave Hayley alone, you will leave my baby alone, or I will take you to court and demand everything you have."

That got his attention. The words seemed to carve through that alabaster mask, revealing the truth beneath. The face she recognised, the one she remembered. The one she had nightmares about.

Oh, he was angry now.

"You think I want that bitch?" he sneered. "All she does is whine. And not half so prettily as you. Come home, baby. Come home and I'll forget her."

"No. You heard me. Leave."

His jaw tightened. His nostrils flared, eyes narrowing to snakelike slits. "It won't change things between you and Hayley, you know. She doesn't like you. I don't even think she loves you."

The words shouldn't hurt this much—not when she'd suspected that fact for a while now, every time her sister's quiet spite and resentment flared a little brighter—but they did. Of course they did. Daniel knew they would.

He pushed his advantage. "Look, babe, you're not thinking straight. You know you need me. You don't know how to live on your own."

God, how had she ever believed that? As if she hadn't been a survivor since childhood?

But before she could respond, she heard Samir say softly, "Laura's not alone."

Which was a mistake. Daniel's gaze flew to Samir, as

sharp and vicious as a shark's teeth. He stared at Samir, not at Laura, as he said, "This guy's not sticking around, babe. Don't be fooled. He probably has a fetish or something." His lips twisted into a smile. "Soon as you drop the kid, he won't be interested."

"Laura?" Samir called.

"Yes?"

"Permission to beat the shit out of your husband?"

Somehow, in the midst of this horrible moment, she managed to laugh. Her giggle sounded like a curse word in church, and that didn't help her composure. Her heart fluttered as she fought to swallow her chuckles. The tension caging her eased, even as she watched a flush of fury stain Daniel's pale skin.

Oh, she loved Samir so much. So fucking much.

"I don't want you to get into trouble," she managed. "He'll call the police."

"Seriously?" Samir's answer dripped disdain. "Wow. That's embarrassing."

Oh dear. The comment, or maybe the casual distaste with which it was said, pushed Daniel's always-precarious temper over the edge. With a strangled roar, he lunged for Samir.

Biting panic ripped through her veins at the sight of her worst nightmare, her greatest fear, swinging at the man she loved. But then something strange happened. Even as she ran forward, the world seemed to slow down. Everything moved like beads of oil floating through water—except for Samir.

So she watched with perfect clarity as he cocked his head, assessed the threat with a flicker of a glance, and stepped aside. So neatly, so simply. Then she watched as he thrust out one foot, and swept Daniel's legs out from under him.

And *then* she watched as her greatest fear went down like a sack of potatoes, landing in a huge heap on the driveway.

Samir's feet were bare. She noticed because he put his heel against Daniel's throat, directly over his windpipe, and exerted enough pressure to have her husband writhing and gasping for air.

"When I get off you," Samir said, "you will have thirty seconds to get up, get in your car, and get the fuck out of my town. Do you understand me?"

Strangled, wheezing screeches were accompanied by weak shudders.

Then Samir lifted his foot slightly and said, "Say yes."

And Daniel actually choked out, "*Yes.*"

"Remember what I said," Laura added. "Stay away from Hayley. Stay away from me. From us. Or I promise you, I will take everything you have. And you know your father will help me."

That familiar green glare found her, but for once, it didn't send a chill down her spine. Maybe because it came from the ground.

"Hey," Samir snapped, pushing his heel into Daniel's throat. "Don't look at her like that. Don't look at her at all."

And, miracle of miracles, Daniel's eyes slithered away.

The miracles didn't stop there, either. They just kept coming. When Samir released Daniel? He dragged himself up and got in his car. *Miracle.*

He reversed out of the drive so fast his tires screeched. *Miracle.*

And he didn't come back. Even though she spent hours tense and waiting for retribution, nothing happened. Samir held her, soothed her, made her eat, and spent all day and night distracting her. And nothing bad happened. Not once. *Miracle.*

And then, in the early hours of the next morning, after he told her for the hundredth time how brave she was, and how well she'd done, and how much he loved her, she managed to tell him the truth.

"I love you too. So much."

Miracle.

CHAPTER SEVENTEEN

THREE MONTHS LATER, the date when Hayley should've arrived came and went. Hayley did not appear. But then, Laura hadn't wanted her to.

Truthfully, Laura barely even noticed her sister's absence, or their mother's, and not just because Samir grew even more attentive as her due date drew near. She barely noticed because, the day after Hayley failed to arrive, Ruth came.

Laura was in the kitchen at the time, stuffing her face with bacon-wrapped dates. Samir was thinking about diversifying the menu at Bianchi's even further—since the pizza had been so successful during the season—and she had graciously agreed to be his test subject. So there she was, nobly and selflessly ingesting her own bodyweight in bacon, when someone knocked at the front door.

Samir went to answer it while Laura continued eating— or rather, shoveling food down her throat at a dangerously high speed. Turned out, he really was a damned good cook. And God, she was always hungry now.

But a familiar voice, bold and blunt, floated into the house and captured her attention. "Ah. You must be the new man. Excuse me."

Then came another voice, less familiar but just as welcome. "Alright, mate? Evan Miller. Nice to meet you. And this is—"

But Laura was already lumbering into the hallway, dates abandoned. She took in the scene all at once: Samir holding the door open, slightly confused but mostly amused. Evan, Ruth's boyfriend, filling the doorway like some big, tattooed, teddy bear of a Viking.

And in front of him, looking tiny between the two men: Ruth. Her dark hair a soft halo, her face predictably unimpressed, her brown skin glowing even more than usual. She was always pretty—it was one of the reasons Laura had once hated her. But since meeting Evan, she'd become fairytale-beautiful through the power of sheer contentment.

"*Ruth!*" Laura cried, sounding so overjoyed she was almost embarrassed. But she hadn't realised until that very moment how badly she needed a friend. Even if that friend was relatively new, highly unorthodox, and had once been the victim of a Laura-led, town-wide hate campaign.

Ruth wasn't one for emotional displays, so she didn't run into Laura's outstretched arms or anything like that. Instead, she pursed her lips in one of her odd, almost-smiles and said, "Oh, I've mucked up my days again. I didn't think you'd be *that* pregnant."

And then, to Laura's everlasting astonishment, the notoriously prickly and secretly shy Ruth Kabbah strode right into the house, past a still-blinking Samir, and gave Laura a hug. It was an awkward, one-armed, wincing hug, but it definitely counted. And it was enough to make Laura burst into tears. Not that it took much these days.

"Oh dear," Ruth said, jerking back as if each salted drop was poisonous.

"You okay, angel?" Samir sounded more amused than concerned, but still, he asked.

"I'm fine! It's fine! I'm just…"

"Leaking," Ruth said grimly. "Like a faulty teapot."

Laura snorted. "What?"

"Oh, never mind. I think some food is in order. Food always helps. Evan brought lasagne." And then, as she dragged Laura into the kitchen: "Oh. You already *have* food." She lowered her voice to a conspiratorial tone. "Yours cooks, too, then? Excellent choice. Very wise, very wise indeed."

Just like that, Laura knew everything from here on out would be absolutely perfect.

THAT NIGHT, after they'd settled Ruth and Evan into the room that should've been Hayley's, Samir pulled Laura into his arms.

They didn't sleep with blankets anymore, because Laura got too hot. She was always too hot, now—but she still needed him to hold her, and honestly, he needed it too. So they slept naked, with a window open, to combat the body heat between them.

Of course, since she was Laura, and she was *naked*, Samir

spent every night hard as hell. And since she was now at that stage of pregnant discomfort where the idea of sex vaguely nauseated her, he was doomed to stay that way until he showered the next morning.

But tonight, he wasn't fighting off inappropriately filthy thoughts. Tonight, he was preoccupied with something... different. Something so huge, he was struggling to drum up the courage to begin

"Ruth is nice," he said, his fingers tracing the stretch-marks on Laura's hips, raised like lace over the silk of her skin. He was a coward, discussing her friends instead of saying what was on his mind, but fuck. Some things were too important for confidence.

"You like her?"

"Of course. She makes you smile." He pressed a kiss to Laura's temple. "Evan's great, too."

"He is, isn't he? I haven't known him long. He only moved to Ravenswood this year."

And there it was, like fate: a perfect segue into the topic Samir was *trying* to broach. "So they haven't been together long, then?"

"Not really. Since Easter, maybe."

"Right." He paused. "But they seem like they've been a couple forever. Years, at least."

"I know. It's funny." Laura gave a happy little sigh. "It's like they were made for each other."

"Do you believe in that?" he asked quickly. "Soulmates, and that sort of thing? Do you think people can be perfect for each other?"

"Ummm..." She hummed out the word, and he winced as he waited for her response. He'd never been so nervous in his life. Which was ridiculous, because he was just feeling her out. Opening a dialogue. Having a reasonable, adult discussion about—

"Maybe," she said. "I mean, I don't think there's only one person for everyone, but I do think that people can be perfectly matched. I think I believe in soulmates. Yeah." She nodded, her hair rubbing against his chin. "I do."

Well, that was something. That would make it easier to argue his case. "I do, too. Honestly, I... Laura, I know this might seem fast. And I know this whole thing between us is, I don't know, unusual. But I feel like you're it for me. I *know* you are."

Slowly, she shifted until their eyes met. The motion brought their bodies even closer, but every inch of his focus was narrowed down to her cool, grey gaze.

Not so cool in this moment. Right now, it looked more like a tempest.

"What exactly are you saying?" she asked softly.

"I just..." He wet his lips, his mouth suddenly dry. "I don't want to push you, but I can't hide this, either. If I thought you were ready for it, I'd ask you to marry me. I'd have asked you weeks ago, to be honest. But right now, I don't know if that would be fair to you. Then at the same time, I don't want you to ever wonder how serious I am about you. Because I know exactly how serious I am, and I can tell you outright. I *am* telling you outright, because soon you'll have the baby, and I know you planned to leave but I —I don't want you to leave. I want you to stay. Here. With me. So I thought you should know that, you know? That I'm not asking, but I will ask. Unless you tell me right now that

I'm doing way too much and you feel, you know, suffocated—"

"Samir," she said gently. He clamped his mouth shut and thanked God she'd stopped him. He'd never babbled so much in his life. His palms might be sweating, actually. "You can't ask me to marry you right now," she murmured.

Even though he'd known that, logically, his heart still staggered a little bit. Not that he'd show it.

But then she said, "I'm still married. Legally, I mean. And even though it means less than nothing to me, I don't want you to propose to a married woman."

His heart stopped staggering and started pounding, louder than a stampede of stallions. "But, to be clear," he said, "once you *aren't* a married woman..."

Her eyes danced like starlight. "Once I'm not a married woman I will go with you to the nearest registry office and become a married woman all over again."

Even as joy suffused him in a bright, brilliant cloud, even as he smiled so hard he hurt his own damn face, Samir shook his head. "A registry office? I don't think so, love."

"What's wrong with a registry office?"

"Oh, nothing. But I want to see sunlight through stained glass windows hitting a white dress..."

"I am not marrying you in a white dress!" He wasn't particularly offended by that, since she giggled as she said it, and slid an absent foot up and down his calf, too.

Still, he feigned outrage as he demanded, "Why the hell not?" Beneath his hand, he felt the baby kick, but that wasn't especially unusual now; the poor kid was up at all hours of the day and night, demanding attention.

"For one thing," she said wryly, "I'm definitely not a virgin."

He shrugged. "But you gave your virginity to me. So the virginity will be present. I have it."

"Oh my God," she snorted. "I can't believe you just said that."

"What? It's true!"

"Did that even count? It lasted, like, five seconds."

What could he say? Fifteen-year-olds weren't noted for their longevity. So, lacking any proper defence, Samir decided to tickle her instead.

"Stop!" she shrieked. "I'll wet myself!"

"I'll stop if you agree to the dress."

"I haven't even agreed to the church!"

"Oh, you shouldn't have reminded me." She squirmed beneath him, gasping out her laughter, but he didn't let up. "The dress *and* the church."

"Samir! I'm serious! I'm going to pee!"

"That's a risk I'm willing to take," he said gravely.

"Fine! Fine, oh my God, stop!"

Even after he let up, she couldn't stop laughing. He started to worry that she actually *would* wet herself—her bladder wasn't particularly sturdy these days. But eventually, she calmed down.

"You're awful," she said, in a voice that suggested he was nothing of the sort.

"I can't help it," he said. "I'm in love."

She didn't reply. Instead, she kissed him so hard he almost forgot to breathe.

CHAPTER EIGHTEEN

A WEEK PASSED UNEVENTFULLY, except for that one night when they built a campfire on the beach and Ruth managed to drop her phone into it. But apparently that wasn't unusual behaviour for her, so 'uneventful' was definitely the word.

They were on the beach again, in the daylight this time, when the big event finally came. Ruth and Evan were actually building sandcastles, and taking it all quite seriously, too. Evan brought out a ruler at one point, which Samir hadn't exactly expected from a blonde behemoth of a blacksmith, but he wasn't really one to judge. Especially since, at that very moment, *he'd* been feeling Laura up quite shamelessly beneath the cover of the ocean.

When she said his name the first time, he thought she was telling him off.

"Sorry," he grinned, because he wasn't sorry at all.

Then she clutched his arm in an iron grip and half-shrieked *"Samir!"* and he realised she wasn't complaining about his hand on her arse.

"What? What is it?"

She'd looked up at him with her teeth bared in an unsettling grimace. "I'm pretty sure I'm having contractions."

"You—your—it—" For at least three seconds, his brain plunged into uselessness as if the power had been cut.

Then, just as suddenly, his mental capacities returned. *"How* sure? How does it feel? For how long? How fast?"

"Quite sure," she said. "It hurts. They started a couple of hours ago—"

"What?"

"And now they're maybe... every ten minutes?"

"What?"

"I didn't want to say anything until I was certain!" she said. "I thought I might be imagining things! Or that it might be Braxton Hicks—"

"Laura, you are forty weeks pregnant. Why the hell would you think it was Braxton Hicks?!"

"It still might be!"

"Woman, I swear to God—"

She interrupted his very serious disapproval with a snort of amusement. "Oh, don't start." But then her face creased into that grimace again, and she huffed out a breath. "Ah. Another one. Oh dear. That was much faster."

"Fuck." He scooped her up into his arms and started wading out of the water. *"Fuck.* Evan!"

And so it began.

❧

IT WAS FORTUNATE, Laura reflected later, that they'd established a plan for this sort of thing just last week. And even better that they'd executed it so well!

She turned to smile at Samir, who was looking very grim. His eyebrows were so... *directional*. Like angry, sharp-edged caterpillars. "We did great," she said, "didn't we?" But her voice sounded slightly slurred. Ah well.

"Yes, angel," he murmured. His hand closed around hers, which was nice—but then she realised that he was taking away her special tube, which was not nice. Laura tightened her grip.

"Get off my magic air," she mumbled.

Finally, his lips quirked into a smile. "It's *gas and air*, my love."

"No! Magic." To prove it, Laura brought the tube back to her lips and sucked down another breath. Oooh, that was nice. Almost nice enough to distract her from the fact that her hips were cracking right down the middle, her vagina was ripping itself in two, her arsehole might be taking the same path, and there was sweat dripping right into her eyes.

Actually, that last part was difficult to ignore. It really stung.

As if he'd read her mind, Samir brushed a cool, dry thumb over her eyelid, sweeping away the beads of moisture. He was so lovely. Lovely! That's why she loved him. She was thinking about how very *much* she loved him when that pesky midwife said, "Laura, I need you to give me a nice big push now, alright?"

Laura took another gulp of magic air. "*No.*"

"Yes, darling, nice big push. Last one. Come on now."

She really didn't want to. She'd been pushing forever,

and it hurt like a motherfucker, and every single time, they *lied* and said it was the last one, and it wasn't. But she felt the oddest sensation down there, as if something was lodged and needed to be released—and *then* Samir took her hand again—not her magic air, just her hand—and murmured, "Push for me, Laura. Please."

So she did. She squeezed his hand so tight that his bones ground together under her grip, and all she could feel was a vicious satisfaction because her own bones were grinding on a much larger scale, and something was definitely ripping her in half, and how dare he sit there comfortably asking her to push? How dare he? How *dare*—

"Keep going, Laura!" The midwife said, sounding rather excited. "One more! One more!"

Lie again. But even though she didn't *want* to push, she kind of felt like she couldn't stop, now. Wasn't that strange? This whole childbirth thing was like smoking bad crack. Not that she'd ever smoked crack. But if she had, it would probably…

"There we go!"

Oh my God. Oh my God. She could hear her baby crying.

Nothing had ever sounded so heavenly.

THE TIME between her son's first cry and the touch of his skin against her own was interminably long. *Ridiculously* long. *Inhumanely* long. But finally, finally, after all sorts of murmurs and mumbles, and the painful, exhausted shove with which she released the afterbirth, and the loudest demands she could muster while floating in a haze of aching soreness, she had him.

She had him. Her baby. Her Bump.

The top of his little head smelled like dried pasta shells. It was delightful. Delicious. She hadn't realised that pasta shells smelled so very lovely until she found the scent nestled in her baby's thick thatch of auburn hair.

Oh, yes, he had hair. He wouldn't open his eyes, and they'd probably be blue anyway, but he had plenty of dark, red hair, and the splotchiest cream-and-raspberry skin, and hands too big for his skinny little body, and a head like a toothless old man's. He was the most beautiful thing she'd ever seen. He fit perfectly under her chin, tucked safely away like a Russian doll, folded in her arms.

She heard Samir's voice, low and assured, as he spoke with a nurse or a midwife or someone. Yes, he said, they were trying to breastfeed, and yes, they had formula ready just in case, and no, Laura didn't mind the blood, or the vernix that lingered on Bump's skin like waxy chalk. They could wash it off later.

Samir came back as she lowered Bump to her breast. The baby snuffled around like a piglet, and she wondered what was supposed to happen now. Some people had trouble, the midwife had told her—it wasn't always plain sailing. But the midwife had also told her to relax and let it happen, so with astonishingly little effort, Laura chilled the fuck out. Must be the magic air.

"Hey," Samir said softly, his hand sliding over her hair.

She smiled weakly up at him, her muscles loose, as if the strings that controlled them had unravelled. Her eyes felt slightly blurry. "Hey yourself."

"How do you feel?"

"I'm... I can't believe I can be so thoroughly uncomfortable in every way, and happier than ever at the same time."

He gave her one of those soul-shaking smiles, and somehow, impossibly, she became even happier. "You did good," he said. "You did really fucking good. And Christ, I'm gonna have to stop swearing, aren't I?"

"Yes, but you can have a pass for now."

He chuckled even as he ran a single finger over Bump's mucky little shoulder. "It's amazing," Samir whispered. "So amazing. That he was in there all this time, coming to life..."

"I know," she whispered back. "Look at him! Look how pretty he is!"

Samir grinned, shaking his head. "Look how pretty *you* are."

"Oh, shut up." She shouldn't be blushing. She was a mother. She had never been so mature in her life as she was now. She *definitely* shouldn't be blushing.

He kissed her cheek. "I love you."

Oh, God, was she blushing. "And I love you."

"And I love Bump."

"But he needs a better name," Laura admitted sadly. She quite liked Bump, to be honest. "A proper name. Like... Fire."

Samir rolled his eyes. "No."

"With a 'y'?"

"You say that like a 'y' makes it better."

"You can't say no to me! I just pushed out a whole baby."

"True," he admitted, his brow creasing into a frown. "Oh! Here's an idea. Let's call Ruth in. I'll let *her* say no to you."

She snorted, then winced as the laughter caused all

kinds of uncomfortable twinges below her waist. That did not bode well. But the midwife didn't seem concerned about anything down there, and really, she couldn't bring herself to care. Not about the state of her nether regions, or the fact that she might be lying in her own blood right now, or even the sleepless nights ahead of her.

Laura couldn't worry about a damn thing. Not with her son lying on her chest and the love of her life holding her hand.

Not when she'd stumbled headfirst into a happiness that she'd once thought she'd never deserve.

EPILOGUE

TWENTY-ONE YEARS LATER

"Phoenix Bianchi!"

They were supposed to hold their applause 'til the end of the ceremony. Samir should've known the twins would ignore that rule.

As their big brother took to the stage in his flowing, black robes, Willow and Sol gave a whoop so perfectly coordinated, it had to be pre-planned.

"Girls!" Laura whispered sharply.

At the iron in their mother's grey gaze, the twins settled down. But that iron melted away like so much city snow when Samir caught his wife's eye over their heads. She gave him a smile that showed every inch of her beaming pride, her pure, unadulterated happiness, and it hit him like an arrow to the heart.

So beautiful. She'd always been so beautiful.

Usually, it took him forever to look away from Laura's smile, from her round, pink cheeks and the creases that cradled her laughing eyes. But today he managed it in record time.

He couldn't miss the sight of his son graduating, after all.

Phoenix shook the presiding officer's hand, standing a head taller than the older man, his auburn hair aflame under the hall's harsh yellow lights. Then, the scroll that symbolised his degree firmly in hand, he strode off the stage.

But not before taking a moment, the barest second, to look out into the crowd for his family. He caught Samir's eye because, though Phoenix loved his mother, he was Samir's boy first.

Samir nodded, knowing his son would understand. *I am so proud of you. Almost too proud to bear.*

Phoenix's smile stretched wider, his cheeks plumping up like his mother's. As if he'd never paused, he left the stage, those robes floating elegantly behind him.

Samir studied his family, the girls in dresses for once and sitting nicely, Laura grinning so wide she might burst. Sometimes he wished he could go back in time and tell his teenage self about this. That he could reassure the Samir who'd once been so full of rage he hadn't trusted himself to speak. That he could say, *One day you'll be surrounded by people who love you. One day you'll have children with Laura Albright, and marry her, and watch your babies become adults, and know that you're capable of contentment, of family.*

But he couldn't time travel. He couldn't tell himself that. And in the end, it didn't matter.

Happiness had been one hell of a surprise.

The End.

AUTHOR'S NOTE

I didn't intend to write this book. The Ravenswood series was *supposed* to be a trilogy... but then

Laura Burne happened.

I knew from the start that Daniel's wife would have to leave him, because Daniel, as we learned in *A Girl Like Her*, is a serial abuser and a piece of human excrement. I couldn't stand to leave a woman—even an imaginary woman—trapped with him. What surprised me, though, was how many of you guys felt the same way. I got so many emails asking what would happen to Laura, how her story would turn out, if she'd get a HEA...

Well, of course, the answer was yes. I'm a romance writer, after all! But I'd planned to slot her HEA into other people's books, as a sort of subplot. Then I realised that she deserved way more than that. *Damaged Goods* is the result.

As always, I want to put some helpful information below:

If you or someone you know is experiencing, or has

experienced, intimate partner violence, I recommend the U.K. charity Women's Aid. They are helpful, trustworthy and genuine.

You can visit their website at https://www.womensaid.org.uk or use their free, 24-hour helpline: 0808 2000 247.

I believe you.

Thank you so much for reading this book. It means a lot.

Love and biscuits,

Talia xx

Read on for sneak peek at Ravenswood book 2, starring Ruth's uptight older sister, Hannah, and the bad boy single dad she'll break every rule for...

UNTOUCHABLE

CHAPTER ONE

Ruth: Evan wants to know if you're coming over for dinner.
Hannah: Aren't *you* supposed to invite me to dinner? Since you're my sister and everything?
Ruth: Do you want his fancy triple-fried chips or not??

As soon as the woman said, "*Excuse* me," Hannah knew there would be trouble.

Maybe it was the way her razor-sharp bullshit-ometer shrieked like a newborn. Maybe it was her years of experience working with kids, AKA masters of pushing their luck and shirking responsibility. Whatever the reason, Hannah's muscles tensed and her smile froze into place before she'd even turned to look at the customer. The customer who, according to her instincts, was about to try some nonsense.

It was the *four-chai-tea-lattes-thanks* blonde from five minutes ago, said chai lattes sitting on the counter in front of her. She pushed her honeyed fringe out of her eyes with a hand that bore a rock the size of Gibraltar. Then she tapped the counter impatiently with one French-manicured claw, just in case the solar flare coming off that ring wasn't enough to alert Hannah to her presence.

"Can I help you?" Hannah asked sweetly, knowing very well that her patience was about to be tested. For the ninth time that day.

God must be punishing me for staring at Emma Dowl's arse in church last week.

"I didn't order these," the woman said. "I wanted plain lattes. Not chai." She spoke with such casual confidence, Hannah almost forgot that she was lying through her expensive teeth. But that blip of confidence passed quickly as Hannah's memory whirred to life.

"No," she said pleasantly. "I gave you exactly what you ordered. You came in..." she glanced up at the clock. "Seven minutes ago. You waited in the queue behind two other people—an older gentleman who ordered a teacake for his wife, and the gentleman in the suit who had a double espresso to go—and when it was your turn you ordered four chai lattes, double shot in two, caramel syrup in the others, one of the double shots 20 degrees cooler. I charged you £14.95, and you paid with a black Santander Select."

The woman stared blankly at Hannah for a moment, like a robot forced to recalibrate. Then her pretty face twisted into an unattractive scowl, and she spat, "I don't appreciate the way you're speaking to me."

Hannah maintained her calm smile and pleasant tone. "I'm sorry you feel that way." She *should* keep her mouth shut and make the damn lattes. Again. But she'd been at work for eight hours, and she'd spent the last three manning the café alone. They were ten minutes from closing. Her shoes pinched and her uniform culottes—yes, *culottes*—dug into her hips awfully, because she'd gained weight again and the damned things didn't come higher than a size 16.

Frankly, Hannah was Not in the Mood.

Apparently, neither was Ms. Latte. She huffed so hard, her fluffy, blonde fringe fluttered. Then she deployed the seven most dangerous words in customer service. "I want to speak to your manager!"

Oops.

Hannah hadn't been a barista for long, but she *had* been waitressing for almost two years before this. And yet, she still hadn't gotten the hang of this whole *be nice to people who don't deserve it* malarkey. She'd never planned on a career that would require her to interact with adults, and certainly not with adults who considered her inherently beneath them. She had *planned* to spend the rest of her life looking after children—preferably babies—because they didn't mind being bossed around or managed, and because they gave credit where credit was due. Give a kid your time, energy and care, and they'd repay you with trust and happiness.

Give an adult the best fucking chai lattes they'd ever tasted, and they'd ask to speak to your manager. Honestly. The ingratitude.

As if summoned by some demonic magic, the man in charge, Anthony-but-call-me-Ant, emerged from his office. He'd spent the last few hours in there doing Super Important Official Things—like playing Candy Crush on his phone—and every time Hannah asked for help, he'd waved her away with a load of supercilious bullshit about how *busy* he was. But the moment he sensed a chance to reprimand her, the tit popped out like a mole from the earth and asked brightly, "Everything okay out here?"

No, Ant, everything is not *okay. It's even less okay now you've shoved your round, shiny, bowling-ball head into things. Why do you exist? Why do you selfishly breathe the precious oxygen that could be better used to sustain a local mischief of rats or perhaps an especially large ferret?*

This was what Hannah thought. Angrily. She could be quite an angry person, at times. Even her depression manifested as anger, which was always fun. But she'd been managing her medication quite wonderfully for the last few months, so she didn't think that was to blame for today's mental fuming. No, this was just her baseline rage talking.

Luckily, Hannah had a lifetime's experience in hiding her baseline rage. Which is how she managed not to fly across the counter and commit a murder when the blonde pouted like a child and said, "No, actually. Everything's not okay. This *person* is being extremely rude to me."

Well. *Extremely* was laying it on a bit thick.

Ant grimaced sympathetically at the customer, then glared at Hannah. "I'm so sorry to hear that. What seems to be the problem?"

"The lady would like to change her order," Hannah said with as much sweetness as she could manage. Which, admittedly, wasn't much.

"You got my order *wrong*," the woman snapped.

I am Hannah fucking Kabbah. I go to the supermarket every week without a shopping list. I once memorised an entire psychology textbook the day before an exam after realising I'd been revising the wrong module for weeks. And guess what? I got an A. I spent the first few years of my professional life keeping multiple toddlers alive. Do you know how hard it is to keep toddlers alive, Ms. Chai Latte? It's really fucking hard. And I was good at it. I do not get things wrong. I do not make mistakes. I do not fuck up FUCKING CHAI LATTES. DO YOU UNDERSTAND ME?

This was what Hannah thought. But what she said was...

Oh. Wait. Shit.

Judging by the looks of utter astonishment on the faces of Ant, the blonde, and the elderly couple sitting over by the window, what she'd *said* was...

Every single word that had just run through her head.

Out loud.

Oh dear.

"*Hannah,*" Ant choked out. He sounded like he was having a heart attack. She didn't blame him. She should be feeling the same way. She should be drowning beneath a tidal wave of shock and panic and embarrassment, frantically grasping for ways to take all of that back and, you know, not lose her job.

But she wasn't. Instead of terrified, Hannah felt peaceful —relieved, actually.

And elated. And free.

Once every few years, Hannah experienced what she privately referred to as a *break.* Whether one chose to interpret that as a pleasant, holiday sort of break, or the more negative *oh-dear-I've-snapped* sort of break was neither here nor there. It didn't matter what she called it or why it occurred, because the outcome was always the same: Hannah's tightly leashed temper broke out, she did something extremely ill-advised, and in the aftermath of her terrible behaviour, she experienced the sort of carefree, unconditional happiness that was usually out of her reach.

Her last break had arguably been the most extreme: she'd smashed a fancy vintage car to pieces with a cricket bat, been arrested, lost her career…. yeah. That one had come at a pretty high price.

But she didn't regret it. Which meant, Hannah realised, that she probably wouldn't regret this, either. And as long as she was riding high on a wave of euphoric adrenaline… might as well enjoy the ride.

Both Ant and the blonde's mouths were hanging open so wide, she could see their fillings. Trying not to smile, Hannah reached beneath her apron and undid the button on her culottes.

Oh, that felt great.

Then she grabbed a little takeaway bag and unscrewed the jar of marshmallows sitting on the counter. They were good fucking marshmallows. She shoved as many into the bag as she could—which turned out to be a decent amount —and popped a few in her mouth, too.

"Hannah?" Ant's smooth, round face was caught comically between astonishment and fury. His pale skin had turned a rather fascinating sort of raspberry colour. "What on *earth* are you doing?"

He sounded like a school teacher preparing to scold a naughty pupil. But Hannah had never been a naughty pupil, and she'd never been scolded at school. Maybe that was why she didn't have the constitution to take it.

"Catch," she said.

"I beg your pardon?!"

She tossed a marshmallow directly into his mouth. Impressive, if she did say so herself.

The blonde gave a little shriek and stepped back, as if she expected a sugary projectile to come her way, too. Smart girl. The elderly couple in the corner, meanwhile, let out an adorable cheer. Hannah loved old people. They were almost as sensible as children, but far more fun. And that was saying something.

"Mumpf aft orffff?!" Ant fumed around the marshmallow wedged in his gob.

"It was a good shot, wasn't it?" Hannah was quite proud. Which made a nice change, actually. She hadn't been proud of herself in a long bloody time.

The feeling grew when she walked around the counter clutching her bag of stolen marshmallows and headed for the door. The old man who'd ordered the teacake winked at her as she passed, and—rather scandalously—she winked back. Good gracious. Perhaps she'd been possessed by a demon with a sense of humour and a spine of hell-forged iron.

"I quit," she called over her shoulder. "You probably gathered that, but men can be rather dense."

"AFFA! TOPF FA—"

"Ant, darling, I can't understand a word you're saying. Don't speak with your mouth full."

The poor man spat out the marshmallow and shouted, "Have you *lost* your *mind*?!"

"Not exactly," she said pleasantly. "It's a free-range sort of arrangement."

~

"Joshua Davis," Nate said, "you spit that out right now."

Josh did not spit it out.

Probably because his older sister, Beth, was giggling helplessly at the sight of the tulip in his mouth. It was Beth who'd told him to eat the damned thing in the first place, and five-year-old Josh thought his seven-year-old sister was the queen of the world, so of course he'd done it.

Perhaps that was the key. Maybe if Nate appealed to the mastermind rather than the loyal solider...

He turned his best parental glare on his daughter and said, "Bethany. Don't feed your brother random plant life."

Beth stuck out her tongue.

Sigh.

The problem was, Nate decided grimly, that his kids weren't scared of him. Not even a little bit. Probably because he sucked at discipline. Like right now, for example —it was 6:30, so they should be in bed reading. Instead, they scurried off deeper into the meadow with squeaky little laughs and shouts of "Bye bye, Daddy!"

Ah, well. At least they were happy.

They'd been through a lot, recently—finding out Grandma was sick, moving across the country, starting a new school. Nate was so happy to see them laughing again, he didn't even notice the stranger walking through the meadow.

Until Josh, and then Beth, barrelled into the distant little figure like a pair cannonballs. Nate watched for a second, frozen, as they all collapsed into the tall grass.

And then he ran.

He'd been loping after the kids like some cartoon monster before, but now he actually sprinted, carving through the distance between them in seconds. It still didn't feel fast enough. He reminded himself that this was Ravenswood, not London, and the person his kids had just bumped into probably wasn't dangerous...

But that didn't really help. For one thing, no matter who it was, they'd all fallen over. The stranger *and* the kids. What if someone was injured? What if Beth had broken her arm again? Or what if the person they'd bumped into was frail or old or something, and now they'd cracked their head open and were currently bleeding out into the grass, and it was all Nate's fault because he couldn't keep his damn kids under control—

"Daddy!" Josh popped up out of the grass like a teary daisy and launched himself into Nate's arms.

Beth picked herself up with far more dignity—she *was* seven, after all—before scurrying away from the person in the grass with a wary look. The kids had this whole *stranger danger* 'thing down. Nate's wife had always been firm about that.

He sank to his knees and wrapped an arm around Beth, his other arm busy holding Josh. Nate ran his hands over all the important parts—heads, ribs, and so on—while he asked questions. "You hurt yourself?"

"No." That was Beth.

"Yes!" That was Josh, using a tone of voice that actually meant, *No, but I need attention.*

He held Josh closer and kissed his head. "There you go, kiddo. You're okay, right?"

Josh sniffled reluctantly.

"Good. Missing any teeth?" He poked at Beth's cheek.

She swatted his hand and giggled. "No. You're silly."

"You sure? Show me." She grinned wide, and he faked a gasp. "Where's your front tooth?"

"It fell out, Daddy!"

"It fell out? Well, where is it? Let's look!"

Josh chuckled. "The other *day*, Daddy! And we left it for the tooth fairy, remember? Not *now*!"

"Ohhh." Nate slapped a hand over his chest and sighed. "Phew! You had me worried!"

The kids shared a look of exasperation. They so pitied their oafish father. Josh wiggled out of Nate's arms and stood, holding Beth's hand as always—and then, as if by agreement, all three of them looked at the stranger on the ground.

She was looking right back, watching their antics with a slight smile on her face—and what a face. It thrust Nate's mind instantly into photographer mode. He saw her as if through a lens, his focus flitting from the way shadow and light danced over her dark skin, to the smooth sweep of her round cheeks into her broad nose, the curve of pouting lips into pointed chin.

She was wearing fuchsia lipstick and her eyes were dark and hot and startling as a shot of espresso. Everything about her was practically daring him to pull out his phone—God, where the fuck was his camera? — and take a picture. Just one. That wouldn't be *too* weird, right? If he explained that she was walking art and it was his job to capture it?

Actually, that would definitely be weird.

"I'm sorry," she said to the kids. "I didn't see you coming. Would you like some marshmallows, to make you feel better? If you're allowed, I mean."

The kids perked up, all supposed injury to person and

dignity forgotten. "Can we, Daddy?" Beth asked. "Can we can we can we—"

"Yeah, yeah," Nate said absently. But the truth was, he'd barely heard the question. Recognition had just hit him in the chest. He'd seen that face most days since he started pre-school for Christ's sake—only back then it had been softer, smaller, childishly undefined. Even when they'd hit their teens, she'd still looked like a little kid. She didn't look like a kid anymore.

But he knew those sharp eyes. The full lips slightly parted by those too-big front teeth. That steady, strident tone...

And the energy snapping about her like an electrical current, as if all that cool composure held back something more intense than he could imagine.

"Hannah," he said, suddenly certain. "Hannah Kabbah. Right?"

"Hello, Nate," she said calmly, as if they bumped into each other on a regular basis. As if this wasn't their first meeting in—God, almost fifteen years? When had he last seen her? The final day of school, maybe? He had no idea. Long enough that it had taken him minutes to recognise a face he'd once seen every day.

Although, he admitted, she did look different now. The same, but... yeah. Different.

Over the past week or so, he'd gotten used to bumping into people he'd once known. None of them had ever been his friends. Every single one had fallen all over themselves to act is if they were long-lost buddies.

But Hannah... he'd actually *liked* her. She hadn't known it, because he'd never told her—and there'd never been any

indication that she liked him, of course. But still. He had the
oddest urge to ask her some clichéd, bullshit question like
How've you been? or *What are you up to these days?* yet she was
busy helping his kids pick out the biggest marshmallows,
barely sparing him a look.

Which, now he thought about it, was just like her.

If she was still the same Hannah he'd known—or even
slightly similar—she wouldn't speak to him until she'd
finished what she was doing. So, Nate sat there, and waited,
and watched. He studied the way she smiled at the kids,
noted the calming effect that her voice seemed to have on
them.

She spoke so slowly—not in a boring way, but as if she
had control of everything around her. As if the world could
very well wait until she finished her sentence. And the kids
reacted like they'd just been pumped full of Calpol and put
down to bed for the night.

He wished any of the nannies he'd been interviewing
recently had been half so effective. Christ, he wished the
nannies he'd been interviewing had actually talked to his
kids at all, instead of talking *at* them.

But he noticed other things, too. Like the hummingbird
flutter of her lashes, and the slight dimple in her chin, and
the careful precision with which she held herself. It was a
precision that spoke of hesitation, of restraint. It made him
wonder.

Once the kids were laden down with marshmallows, she
finally looked up. At him. It felt sort of like being electro-
cuted. He had no idea why. Maybe that was why he blurted
out, "We should catch up."

The kids shared a meaningful look at those foreboding

words. Beth mumbled around a mouthful of marshmallows, "Daddy, can we go and play?"

"Sure. Don't go past that tree, okay?" He pointed to a nearby beech, close enough that he'd have them in his line of sight, well-lit by a streetlight.

"Okay!" They ran off together, sticky hands clasped, cheeks stuffed full of marshmallows like hamsters with grain.

Leaving him and Hannah on their knees, Nate suddenly realised, staring at each other like lemmings.

"Catch up?" she repeated faintly, with the sort of tone he might use to say *"Eat mould?"*

"Uh… yeah." He ran a hand through his hair. Christ, he needed a haircut. He stood, and she followed suit, which made him realise how short she still was. Or maybe she just seemed that way because he was tall. Whatever. He should've stayed on his knees. He felt like some kind of ominous, oversized thing, looming over her in the half-light.

She cocked her head slightly as she looked at him, like a bird considering an unsuspecting worm. The shadows shifting over the smooth planes of her face were giving him ideas. He hadn't shot anyone professionally in years, but all of a sudden, he could see a thousand images in his mind's eye. Something about her…

"I don't think we have much to catch up on," she said.

Nate forced himself to focus on the conversation, since he was the one who'd started it. "We don't?"

"No. I know everything there is to know about you."

UNTOUCHABLE: Available Now

ABOUT THE AUTHOR

Talia Hibbert is an award-winning, Black British author who lives in a bedroom full of books. Supposedly, there is a world beyond that room, but she has yet to drum up enough interest to investigate.

She writes sexy, diverse romance because she believes that people of marginalised identities need honest and positive representation. She also rambles intermittently about the romance genre online. Her interests include makeup, junk food, and unnecessary sarcasm.

Talia loves hearing from readers. Follow her social media to connect, or email her directly at hello@taliahibbert.com.

CPSIA information can be obtained
at www.ICGtesting.com
Printed in the USA
LVHW111725041019
633216LV00002B/368/P